A Hallie Marsh Mystery

San Francisco, Paris, New York, Washington, Santa Fe

# Merla Zellerbach

# Dying to Dance

firefall™

First Edition: November 2012

cover design: BJR/EB

ISBN:  9780915090457  (hardcover)

FIREFALL EDITIONS
Canyon California 94516-0189

literary@att.net
www.firefallmedia.com

# Novels by Merla Zellerbach

*Dying To Dance*

*Love To Die For*

*The Missing Mother*

*Mystery of the Mermaid*

*Secrets in Time*

Firefall Editions

*Rittenhouse Square*

Random House

*Sugar*

*Cavett Manor*

*Love The Giver*

*The Wildes Of Nob Hill*

Ballantine

*Love In A Dark House*

Doubleday

To Lee, who dances through life with me…

My warmest thanks to my friend and brilliant publisher, Elihu Blotnick, to Dr. Robert Liner & Judy Bishop for medical know-how, to Dr. Gordon Lithgow, molecular gerontologist at the Buck Institute for Research on Aging, and to Mary & Bill Poland, strong supporters of the Buck Institute.

More thanks to textile expert/opera singer Margot Schevill and architect Adolph Rosekrans, to beautiful cover girl Susan Tamagni, to Registered Dental Hygienist Marian Brenner, to my dedicated pals at Compassion & Choices, and to my children, Linda & Gary Zellerbach, my grandchildren Laura and Randy Zellerbach, and to so many friends and family members who encourage these mysterious goings on.

# DYING TO DANCE


## PART 1

## Chapter 1

*Late afternoon*
**February 4th, 2011**

"I'D LIKE to learn to dance, and possibly meet a financially independent woman. Have I come to the right place?"

The well-dressed gentleman shifted his weight uneasily. He didn't believe in deception. If the man didn't like his motives, he'd go elsewhere.

Tobias Miller saw no reason to take offense. The stranger got points for honesty. He was also tall, with a thick patch of gray hair and matching moustache, attractive, well-spoken, and of the gender the San Francisco Dance Studio desperately needed in its intermediate classes.

He motioned for the visitor to come inside. "My name's Tobias Miller. I'm the owner here. And you are?"

"Sam Butler." He presented his card. "I'm a molecular gerontologist. I do research on aging."

"Fascinating!"

"Unfortunately, my wife Olivia died two months ago. We were together thirty-four years. I enjoy female companionship, but not the kind my daughter Lina calls 'high maintenance' – the ones who expect to be wined, dined, and showered with gifts. I'm not poor, but after putting three daughters through college, I'm not rich, either."

"May I ask if you're over forty?"

"I'm fifty-four, and I don't care about a woman's age, as long as she's kindhearted and intelligent. You can check my credentials online."

"Have you done much dancing?"

"Olivia and I did the two-step, but that's about it. I'd like to learn something new. For instance, when young people stand apart and bounce around to the music. I don't know how to do that."

"Freestyle – it's easy and you'll love it. Our one-hour afternoon classes teach basic footwork, and the students rotate partners during the session. It's a low-key learning environment."

"Excellent!"

"And if I may boast a bit, we're unique in the dance world in that we teach everything from Hula to Hip-hop, and all our instructors offer videos so the students can practice at home. It's especially helpful for beginners."

"That would be I."

Tobias raised an eyebrow and went on. "The intermediate and advanced sessions are more challenging, but there's still no pressure. Aside from the videos, which are optional, there's nothing to buy, no books, no props, no uniforms. All you need are some loose, comfortable clothes, and shoes with a little support."

Sam nodded. "Sounds fine. You see, Olivia knew she was dying, and it was actually her idea that I should go to dancing school and perhaps meet some nice women. We never had much of a social life. Our friends were not names you'd find in the newspapers. She was a poet, and the people we saw were mostly scientists and writers. If I sound like an intellectual snob, it's because I am."

"So I've noticed. Since you're a highly intelligent man, you may already know that dancing improves brain function. Impartial studies show that trained dancers process information better and have increased ability to remember facts."

"I'm not here to improve my brain."

Tobias laughed. "Okay, you're being honest with me, I'll be honest with you. I'll definitely check your credentials. You could be a clever con man who's set up a fake website, and likes to prey on rich widows. I have to protect my clients and if I find out you're not who you say you are, I'll press charges and send you to jail."

"Fair enough." Sam Butler smiled. The man spoke his mind; he liked that and would do the same. "Your prices are quite steep. But Olivia had a friend – Carlie something – who took lessons here and recommended it."

"Carlie Gaines, a lovely young woman."

"She owned a dress store. Olivia sometimes shopped there. I'd like to meet her. My daughter wants me to run an ad or sign up with an online matchmaker, but I've no time for that nonsense."

"Come into my office." Tobias led the way. "We can discuss what would best suit your needs and I'll take your information and a hundred dollar deposit. If you change your mind or lie on your application, I won't refund a cent. Do we have an agreement?"

"Absolutely, Mr. Miller. And may I count on your discretion?"

"Indeed you may, Mr. Butler. I believe we do understand each other."

— Chapter 2 —

SAM BUTLER hurried to his car, parked three blocks from
the Dance Studio on busy Union Street. The building, Tobias
recalled, was built in the 1950s. A onetime department store,
it was rebuilt in 1972 and had grown to become the Bay
Area's most prestigious and successful dance center.

When the owner died in 2002, Tobias, one of the
instructors, had managed to buy the school with several
investors. He later bought out his partners and promptly replaced the staff with the country's best professional teachers,
"all of whom," he'd explained, "have won major prizes and
awards. As you'll see, we're wholly dedicated to quality and
professional ethics."

Sam wondered if taking on a client whose admitted
goal was to meet "Ms. Right" compromised those ethics, but
no, Tobias had assured him, almost all their students came
looking to make new friends; Sam just happened to be more
up-front about it. He might have been even more "up-front"
if he'd been sure of the meaning of that expression. The term
sounded vaguely pornographic, and he had yet to master
modern jargon.

His reasons for enrolling in the school, however, were
not limited to making new friends. Granted, he was lonesome. He wouldn't mind meeting a woman who had brains,
abilities, a love of the arts, and wasn't after a man strictly to
support her.

But he also wanted to work off a small roll of fat
around his waist, and *do* something while he exercised, which
otherwise seemed a waste of time. And most definitely, he

needed to learn to dance. His middle daughter was marrying her gay partner in Massachusetts later that year, and she'd asked him to give her away, adding that he'd be expected to whirl both brides around the floor. None of that had seemed worth mentioning to Tobias.

After expressing interest in an "Over Forty" class Tuesday and Friday evenings from five to six, he'd been surprised to see Tobias insert a disk into a machine, take his arm, walk him to the floor and ask him for a dance. "Nothing personal," he'd said, "I'd just like to see what you know. You lead."

Thinking back, Sam laughed to himself as he climbed into this car. Tobias was about five-foot-six, balding, with a prominent paunch, yet amazingly light on his feet. He'd taught Sam the box step, then complimented him for learning it on the spot. Thank goodness no one had walked in while the two men were waltzing around the ballroom.

"You have promise," Tobias had concluded. "Let's make a deal."

— Chapter 3 —

"DAD, FOR GOD'S SAKE, you've signed up for *what?*"

"Dance classes – Tuesdays and Fridays after work." Sam Butler spoke softly into his iPhone. Lina Butler Holmes was the oldest of his three girls, and quite possessive of her newly-widowed father.

After all, he was handsome, charming, brilliant, and she was convinced every unattached woman he met would be after him. Men were so gullible – so easily influenced by a woman, especially if she were inclined to bestow sexual favors. Lina couldn't let her father fall prey to some horny vampire.

There were complications, though. Married to a pediatrician, mother of two young children, with a part-time teaching job at a preschool, Lina had little time to police her father. If only she could attend dancing school with him – but she couldn't.

"I was about to sign up for the beginner class," he went on, "when Tobias, the owner, invited me for a waltz. So I stepped on his toes for a while, he counted the beat in my ear, and finally, he pronounced me agile enough to join the intermediate group."

Lina restrained a giggle at the thought of her ultra-serious father twirling around the dance floor with a man. "Cool, Dad," she managed to say.

"You'll be proud of me," he continued. "It's a first class school. They even sponsor a nonprofit called 'Dance Kids,' where they teach kids poise and social interaction through dancing."

"Wonderful."

"Besides," he went on excitedly, "They need men badly, so I'm only paying for one class. I can attend any of the others whenever I want – and I don't have to pay a cent!"

Big effing deal, she thought. If they need men so badly, he shouldn't be paying anything; they should be paying him. But he had no idea how to bargain. A workaholic all his adult life, he'd been wedded to a job he loved. Her mother had made the major family decisions, done the shopping, chosen their cars, their clothes, planned vacation trips, and bought and furnished their house.

Later, when the last daughter had gone off to college, Olivia had arranged their move into a charming apartment in Pacific Heights, an upscale residential district.

As far back as Lina could remember, her father was spending long days at his laboratory in the Buck Institute for Research on Aging in Novato, a short distance across the Golden Gate Bridge in Marin County.

She knew that no matter what time of day she tried to call him, Sam Butler was always buried in his research, looking for ways to prevent age-related diseases such as Alzheimer's and Parkinson's, and searching for secrets to slow the aging process. The Institute's goal, he once told her, was to extend what they called "healthspan" – the healthy years of life.

All Lina knew was that he'd learned how to make microscopic worms live longer by reducing their stress levels. How much stress could a microscopic worm have? And if her father was as brainy as everyone said, why was he so naïve about everything else?

"That's wonderful, Dad. Just be careful of the women you meet. Lots of hungry piranhas out there."

"Don't worry, sweetheart," he assured her. "I can take care of myself."

— Chapter 4 —

As soon as he clicked off the phone, Sam felt a wave of loneliness. During the week, he rarely left his lab before six in the evening, but now that he had five o'clock dance classes, he'd have to change his routine.

When friends teased him about his preoccupation with the nematode worm, *Caenorhabditis elegans,* he'd simply reply that the "little guys" held some of the mysteries of aging. He'd discovered a range of factors that lengthened life in the worms, and he was determined to learn all of their secrets – and how they could apply to humans.

In rare free hours, he'd catch up on the *New York Times* and various scientific and medical journals. Having started out to be a physician, he'd spent two years in medical school before deciding he preferred research and lab work to dealing with sick people.

It was a wise decision, one he'd never regretted. Work was his passion, and the days passed quickly. Evenings and nights were when he most missed Olivia.

Before she died of leukemia, Olivia had insisted that she didn't want him to mourn her. "Pull your head out of the sand and look around," she'd said, trying to smile. "There's a whole big world out there, beyond your laboratory. There's more to life than worms."

He'd held her and cried. The memory brought new tears, along with his recollection that he'd promised to get out of his rut. But where to start? He wasn't about to go to a bar or a nightclub, or God forbid, a strip joint, but he was hungry. Maybe it was time to find a food source other than the counter at Mel's Drive-in – even if they did have great burgers.

## — Chapter 5 —

"Elm" was a popular restaurant not far from Sam's Jackson Street apartment. He and Olivia had gone there often, and he remembered a bar area apart from the tables. Did he dare dine alone?

Despite apprehensions, a quick change of shoes, shirt and slacks reinforced his desire to keep his promise to his late wife. After leaving his car with the valet, he entered the restaurant, and to his surprise, was greeted warmly.

"Wonderful to see you, Dr. Butler," gushed a young woman. "I'm Megan, the host. My condolences about your wife. We've missed you."

"Thank you. Nice to see you, too, Megan."

"Umm – are you meeting someone?"

"No, that's the problem. I'm alone and I don't know if I should even be here."

"You should definitely be here. May I seat you at the bar counter? Many of our customers come in alone. And I can pretty well guarantee you won't be alone for long."

"Oh, I don't want to pick anyone up."

She smiled. "I just meant you'll find people to talk to if you want to. If you don't, they won't disturb you. Follow me, please."

A few minutes later, Sam checked the menu and realized everything on it looked good. Stauffers' dinners and hamburgers would keep him alive, but left much to be desired. He ordered a Caesar salad, duck confit, and a glass of Chardonnay – for starters.

Then he began to study his surroundings. The lights were dim, which always pleased Olivia. She hated her few wrinkles. Rust-colored walls displayed a collection of modern paintings he neither liked nor understood.

"You don't have to understand modern art," one of his friends had explained, walking him through a gallery. "Just look at the work and feel whatever you feel."

What he felt, he remembered thinking, was amazement that artists could get away with calling a bunch of lines and scribbles "art." One painting with a four-figure price tag was a large white canvas with a blotch of green. Another was a multicolored penis with a human head. The listing had a gold star – someone had actually bought that piece of crap!

He might not be as worldly as his contemporaries, but he knew art, especially the French Impressionists. Where was Monet? Degas? Matisse? Where were the old masters when you needed them? Those people didn't try to con you.

— Chapter 6 —

THE BAR COUNTER WAS SHORT, with seats for eight. Two women were at one end. Sam sat two places away, and a man sat at the other end. The gentleman looked over at Sam and smiled.

Not knowing what else to do, Sam smiled back. Oh, Lordy, what had he done? The man was coming right towards him!

"Pardon the intrusion," said the stranger, handing him a card. "My name's Dan Casserly and I'm the editor-in-chief of *CityTalk* magazine. One of my writers did a story on the increase in, well, mature people dining alone, and I need a bit more information. Would you mind if I sat here?"

"No – no, please do." Sam sighed with relief. The man wore a gold wedding ring and didn't appear to be homosexual. "I don't know how I could help you, Mr. –" He glanced down at the card. "Casserly?

" 'Cas' is fine."

"To be honest, I'm a new widower and this is my first time dining out. Olivia – my wife – before she died, she made me promise not to sit home reading every night."

"What a kind, caring woman she must have been. Please accept my condolences. This must be difficult for you."

"How nice that you understand. I shouldn't take up your time, though. Perhaps those two women at the end of the counter can help with your story."

"I'd like to get your story, Sam, if I'm not intruding on your first night out. Could we move to that booth in the corner?"

"Oh, I don't know –"

Cas reached in his pocket for his wallet, and opened it. "See this gorgeous creature? She's my wife, Hallie. She keeps her own name – Hallie Marsh. We've been married a little over a year now, and I adore every inch of her magnificent self. Does that help?"

"Frankly, I guess it does." Sam gave a self-conscious shudder. "I'm not very interesting, though."

"I'll be the judge." Cas motioned to the bartender, pointed to the table, and dropped a bill on the counter.

# — Chapter 7 —

An hour and two Chardonnays later, Sam was still spilling his life story, leaving out few details, grateful to have someone to talk to – someone who asked questions and seemed truly interested in him and his worms.

For his part, Cas was delighted. Sam was inspiring a completely different story – a tale of a man of science, a dedicated researcher and sheltered widower entering a new phase of his life.

There must be hundreds, Cas thought, maybe thousands of men like him – men of all ages who'd lost their partners, or their jobs, or their families, and were suddenly facing life alone. They didn't have the network of friends most women have, and they weren't homeless, just scared and lonely.

He would start the piece with Sam, then assign a reporter to seek similar subjects. Perhaps knowing how others overcame problems would benefit those in the same situation.

Noting that Cas didn't drink, Sam wondered if his companion had health problems, and was pleased when Cas clicked off the tape recorder and began answering questions about himself. He explained that he was a "friend of Bill W's," a reference to Bill Wilson who co-founded Alcoholics Anonymous. "Friends" was a euphemism for the support group.

"I joined AA years ago, but never followed the rules until I met my wife," Cas went on. "In 2008, I was lecturing aboard a cruise ship and Hallie and her girlfriend Kris were passengers. When I first spotted Hallie, she knocked my eyes out. I was smitten before we even met. But man, was she snooty! I kept trying to talk to her, and she kept telling me to get lost. One day she came up to me and told me that stares cost a buck apiece. I told her I'd take five, slipped a bill in her pocket and walked away."

"Did she keep it?" asked Sam, fascinated.

"Let's say it paid off." Cas laughed and continued, "But it wasn't easy. She thought I was some cheap Romeo looking for a quickie shipboard romance. Then one day her friend Kris dragged her to a lecture, and lo and behold, I was the speaker. The Cruise Director introduced me, rattling off my various journalism awards and honors, my background as Bureau Chief of the Associated Press in Washington, and my work as editor-in-chief of *City Talk*."

"Impressive."

"I hoped it would be. When I saw Hallie and her traveling companion, Kris, sitting in the second row. I decided to give my number one speech, a pitch for democracy, freedom, patriotism. It usually got me a standing ovation, and that time was no exception. Suddenly I was the ship's hero."

"Bet that got her attention." Sam looked admiringly at his new friend – about six-foot-two, dark brown hair streaked with gray, manly features and intense brown eyes peering through horn-rimmed glasses. "You're a good-looking man, Cas. I'm sure it didn't take long after that."

"It wasn't easy. She had a minor physical situation she thought would turn me off, but I was already so taken with her, it didn't make the least bit of difference."

Hallie's double mastectomy was something he rarely thought or talked about. Boobs weren't exactly a novelty, he'd told her, and he'd had "more than I could handle – so to speak," in his bachelor days. She was healthy and cancer-free, and that was all that mattered to him.

"Do you have children?" asked Sam.

"Not yet. We're working up to it. Hallie owns a PR – Public Relations firm, and likes to solve crimes in her spare time. She's pretty good at it, too, when she stays out of trouble. Her mother bought us a house last year, and now that we've moved in, she's busy fixing everything up. So that's it, my whole life story." He reached for his camera. "May I get a quick picture?"

"Why – I guess so."

Click, click. "I'll send you a copy, Sam. How do I reach you?"

"I'm in the phone book. Address and all."

"Great. Thanks for the interview." He shook hands and slid out of the booth. "I'll get the check and have the waiter bring you some coffee. Take it easy driving home."

— Chapter 8 —
*Two Weeks Later*

WHAT A PLEASANT SURPRISE that first dance class was, Sam Butler thought, as he stood over the sink in the men's locker room. Jeff Donegan, the hyperactive ballroom instructor in skin-tight pants, had made sure each of the eight women in the class had a chance to dance with Sam, one of his two male students. By the end of the lesson, Sam felt confident that he was doing at least a passable fox trot.

After wiping the sweat off his forehead, he ran a comb through his hair, noticed that it needed cutting, and grabbed his sport coat. "Goodnight, Sweetheart" was still playing in his head when he left through the school's front door.

The five o'clock lesson had ended promptly at six. The streets were still light. As he started to walk to his car, a voice called his name. He turned to see a dark-haired woman hurrying towards him.

"Hello," she said, smiling, "I'm Polina. Remember the rumba? The instructor said I wiggled my pelvis too much."

"Yes, of course." How could he forget? She was unusually pretty, and he'd have to have been blind not to notice her tight leotard and abundant cleavage. But she looked to be in her twenties, and much too young for him.

"May I invite you for a cup of coffee?" she asked.

"That's kind of you, Polina —"

"Don't say no, please? I really feel the need to talk to someone."

"Is there a problem?"

"Yes," she said. "There is. Is this your car? I live close by, in the Marina district. If you'd drive me home, I'd be forever grateful."

Sam swallowed nervously. Although he'd mentally prepared for several possibilities in the dance class, a young woman in distress wasn't one of them. "Okay, I guess." He opened the car door for her.

"Thanks. You have nice manners."

She directed him down a series of hills. "Sam," she said, "could you pull over a second? I think the Golden Gate Bridge is the most beautiful, graceful thing I've ever seen. Do you agree?"

"I don't know. I drive across it to work every day but I've never taken the time to look at it." He stopped in front of a driveway and rolled down his window. "You're right, Polina. Visually – architecturally – it's a brilliant amalgamation of practicality and design. I'm just beginning to learn what an amazing city this is."

"You should see it from my bedroom window."

Was that an invitation? No, how crude of him to be thinking that way. He quickly moved on, her directions taking him to a white stucco house with blue shutters, not far from Crissy Field, the popular walkway along the Bay. He braked at the curb, hoping she wouldn't ask him in.

"You can leave your car in the driveway."

"I'm afraid I can't come in."

"Please?" She stared imploringly. A lone tear rolled down her cheek. "I live with my grandmother. She won't hear us. She'll be sleeping."

Damn, he thought. What did she want from him?

"Never mind," she said, sniffing. "I understand. You just totally don't like me."

"Polina, I – oh, hell." He climbed out and came around the car to help her out. "I can't stay long. I have to be somewhere at seven."

"You're an angel, Sam, I'm so grateful."

## — Chapter 9 —

THE CLOCK STRUCK SEVEN, and Sam sat on Polina's couch, staring at his watch. He didn't really have to be anywhere, but it was a good excuse to leave.

He'd heard her story. Her parents brought her here from Russia when she was two. They went back to Russia, leaving her with her grandmother, who raised her. She was supposed to get educated, then return to Russia. But she was American now, and didn't want to go back, so she'd stayed. Her eyes filled with tears.

The problem, she explained, was that someone was stalking her. Someone had tried to run her over. Someone was calling her at odd hours, and hanging up. Her father in Russia used to be KGB, now he was a police officer. She was sure someone was trying to scare her – perhaps because of her father. The Russian mob was everywhere. Yes, she'd talked to the police. No, they weren't doing anything. No, he didn't want coffee, tea, or a ham sandwich. Yes, she knew he had to leave.

"I'm so frightened," she said, "Is there any way I can convince you to stay a little longer?"

His patience had run out. He rose and headed for the door. "I've stayed too long already, Polina. Talk to the police if you're frightened. Goodnight."

"Wait!" She reached for his arm. "Look!"

He turned to see her unbuttoning her blouse. The leotard was underneath. This time the invitation was unmistakable, even to a naïve scientist.

With a sigh, Sam released the doorknob and faced

her. "Look here, young lady, I'm not interested in having sex with you. But I have three daughters your age and I'd be happy to stay a few minutes and talk to you about what you're doing with your life."

"My life's just fine," she snapped, raising her chin and buttoning her blouse. "I don't need a lecture. Get lost."

— Chapter 10 —

AFTER two glasses of Pinot Noir to complement his Stauffer's meat loaf, Sam sat in his kitchen feeling mellow, and reflecting on Polina's behavior. The experience was a lesson, he decided – a warning that this new generation had different manners and morals. He knew that wise people didn't dwell on negatives, and he tried not to over-analyze Polina's invitation, but he needed some distraction to put it behind him.

Thinking back to the dance class, he was grateful that Jeff, the instructor, had introduced him to the other students, especially Carlie Gaines, a lively redhead Jeff whisperingly referred to as "eye candy." Sam liked her immediately and was touched by her kind words about his late wife.

Carlie was in her mid-thirties, he guessed, with symmetrical features, translucent skin, a slim waist and hips. Attractive as she was, he was sure Olivia hadn't expected him to be interested in her. Besides the age difference, high fashion clothes, scarlet nails, perfectly-coiffed hair and expensive-looking jewelry told him that she was precisely the "high-maintenance" type he wanted to avoid.

Nevertheless, he was lonesome for female company, and had several "domestic" questions he thought only a woman could answer. He debated the pros and cons of inviting her to dinner, then decided to chance a call. When she answered, he explained that Olivia wanted him to get to know her, and that she reminded him of his daughters.

"I hear you, Sam Butler," Carlie said, laughing. "Olivia was a dear woman. She didn't want you to be lonely, and she knew you well enough to know that you wouldn't be after me for anything but friendship. Guess I'm not your type."

"I'm too old for you," he said, relieved.

"Please relax, Sam. I adore the idea of having an attractive, well-educated male escort who has no interest in me other than companionship. What time will you pick me up tomorrow?"

— Chapter 11 —

CARLIE WAS WAITING in the lobby Saturday evening when Sam drove up the pathway to her condominium building. She waved, and motioned him not to get out; the doorman escorted her to his car and opened the door.

"Hello," he said, smiling. How pretty she was! Long auburn hair complemented her soft pink complexion and wide brown eyes. She wore little makeup, or else it was so expertly applied it was invisible. A beige sweater, skirt, and tan boots showed off her trim form. "Ever hear the phrase, 'A thing of beauty is a joy forever?' "

"Shakespeare?"

"Keats. And it fits you."

"That's very gallant." Her face lit up as she settled

into the seat and touched his arm. "I'm so glad you called me. Are you hungry? I'm starved. There's a good restaurant nearby if you like Chinese food."

"Just direct me."

Moments later, they were sitting opposite each other in the corner of a brightly-lit room. Colorful posters and Oriental music added atmosphere; the noise level was high but bearable. An Asian server offered drinks, and Sam was pleased to let Carlie do the ordering.

"They don't serve pheasant-under-glass here," she announced, as they awaited their wine. "About the only thing under glass is the tablecloth. But I sense you're not big on frills."

"You're right, Carlie. I was brought up to be direct. Olivia used to try to teach me small talk, but I never got the knack."

"I like that. So let's make big talk. Tell me about your fascinating self."

He laughed. "Ladies first. Where were you born?"

"Fair enough. I came into the world at the Cedars-Sinai Medical Center in West Hollywood. My Mom was a financial wizard who invested wisely, Dad was a handsome bank clerk, and they had a good marriage at first. I won't bore you with details, but they had me, an only child, and divorced when I was seven. Dad married his French girlfriend and moved to France. That didn't last, he lost his job, and became the bum and con artist he is today. I don't have anything to do with him."

"That's sad."

"*C'est la vie.* Fifteen years ago, in 1996, I turned

twenty-five and inherited a trust fund from my late mother."

"That makes you – forty?"

"*Just* forty," she said with a giggle. "I don't need to work, but I've spent half my life trying to earn a living. I love to dance, and I studied ballet but wasn't good enough to make it a career. Then I went to law school. I gave up after two failed bar exams, tried my hand at interior design, but that didn't work either, so I invested in a dress shop that went broke. I'm dating my lawyer and he thinks I should spend more time smelling the roses. But I can't be idle, so I'm looking for something else to flunk at."

"You don't look like a failure to me. The dress shop – that's where you met Olivia?"

"Yes, I didn't know her well but I truly liked her. After the shop went under, I signed up for the dance class to keep in shape while I seek a new profession."

"Have you ever married?"

"No, but – well, confidentially, I'll be announcing my engagement soon. When I do, I want you to meet my fiancé. Our next date will be a threesome, okay? Now it's your turn to talk, Sam."

Respecting her desire not to discuss her groom-to-be – could it be the lawyer she was dating? – he reminisced about his marriage, his pride in his daughters, his passion for work. He told of the time Olivia teased him, saying, "Some men have mistresses – guess I'm lucky to marry a man who loves worms!"

He and Carlie laughed, ate heartily, talked non-stop, and ended the evening with a warm hug. Sam would respect her request that their next dinner date include her fiancé –

but he was secretly disappointed that she wasn't interested in seeing him alone again. After all, a fourteen year age difference wasn't that big a deal, was it?

— Chapter 12 —

THE DELIGHTFUL Chinese dinner and a restful Sunday had reinvigorated Sam Butler, who awoke Monday morning eager to start the week. Surprised by his strong reaction to Carlie, he was pleased to realize he could again be attracted to a woman – but then, who wouldn't respond to such a charmer, even one promised to someone else?

Reality, however, was hard to ignore. How could a young, socially-aware woman be interested in an older man who was unsophisticated, unworldly, an awkward dancer, and not the least bit rich?

With a sigh, he tried to get her out of his mind, at the same time reminding himself of his promise to Tobias. He had offered to attend as many evening classes as he could.

Glancing at the Monday dance schedule, he saw that although it was a holiday, Presidents' Day, two lessons would be in session, including "Hip-Hop for Beginners" late that afternoon. What was hip-hop, he wondered? Maybe it was that twisty dance-alone step that all the young people were doing. He had to push himself to try new things.

The class took place in a small room off the main ballroom. Instructor Jennifer, a petite woman with plain features, greeted him warmly. "I'd like you to meet Sam," she told her four students, all females. "Isn't he brave to want to learn hip-hop?"

The young women, teenagers, he suspected, gave tentative smiles. He groaned mentally, and moved to the rear of the room. This was not what he expected.

"All right, class, remember what we did last time? You just watch, Sam, and as soon as you feel ready to join us, please do so."

The teacher stood facing the front of the ballroom; the students lined up behind her. As she began to dance, she set the beat: "Step back, step back, a one-foot hop, and a two-foot jump. Arms bent high, hands face floor, twist the body and try once more. Step back, step back..."

Sam stood watching for thirty seconds. That was all it took. With a nod to Jennifer, he said a quick, "Excuse me, wrong room," and left.

Relieved to escape the teeny-boppers, he wandered down the hall into a Viennese waltz class. Brigitte, the instructor, was so delighted to have an attractive male partner, she kept him moving the whole hour. He found her helpful and professional, and promised to come back.

The next evening, despite his discomfort at having to face Polina again, he returned to his Tuesday swing-dance class. She was not there. After the session, he approached the instructor. "Aren't we missing someone?" he asked casually.

Jeff's face tightened. "Polina Belnikov. I've been trying to reach her all weekend. She gave me some sob story about her sick grandmother and I fell for it and lent her my car. I haven't seen her since and the phone number she gave me is disconnected. I hope she's not skipping out on me. But I've a hunch...she's disappeared."

*PART 2*

# — Chapter 13 —
## *Two weeks later*

HALLIE MARSH sat at the breakfast table, reading the latest issue of *CityTalk* magazine. Cas had told her about his interview with Sam Butler, and one of his reporters had spent several evenings searching for other men dining out alone.

He'd found quite a few. Many were travelers, but a surprising number were exactly what he was looking for, city dwellers with tales to tell. Some refused to talk, some were brief, some talked too much. But in general, their stories made good copy.

As she was flipping the pages to the next feature, the phone rang. Caller I.D. said, "Anonymous," which always irked her. If the calls were legitimate, why wouldn't people want to be identified? She picked up the receiver.

"Mrs. Casserly?"

"Yes. Hallie Marsh, actually."

"My name's Sam Butler. You don't know me –"

"The famous Sam Butler I just read about in *City-Talk?*"

He laughed. "The very same. Your husband did a wonderful job. I'm calling to thank him. Is he about?"

"No, he's out of town at the moment. I'm glad you were pleased. I'll tell him you called."

"That would be…nice."

She sensed his hesitation. "In the interview you said you were starting dance lessons, Mr. Butler. How did that go?"

"The dancing's going fine, thanks…"

"But?"

"A small problem. I won't bore you."

"I love hearing other people's problems. Didn't Cas tell you I'm snoopy?"

"He said you like to solve crimes. I'm not sure this is a crime."

"Sam," she said, "pardon my use of your first name, but what's going on that has you concerned?"

The woman was snoopy, all right, yet she seemed sincere. And he needed to talk. "Okay. One of our dance students is missing – a young Russian woman who thinks the Russian mob might be after her. She borrowed the instructor's car and he can't reach her. I said I'd help him find her, but frankly, I don't want to get involved."

"That's not boring at all. Did you know her well?"

"I only saw her once, my first evening in the class. She asked me to give her a ride home – then insisted I go inside. She tried to seduce me and I left in a hurry. That's all I know. Jeff – the instructor – said she doesn't answer her phone and her mail is returned."

Hallie's ears perked up. "Has anyone been to her house?"

"Yes. The people who live at the address she gave the school, never heard of her."

"But you drove her home?"

"That was to a different house, not the address on her registration. I'm tempted to go back to that first house, but I barely know Polina, and it's none of my business. If she's there, I don't want to see her and get trapped again."

"You won't," she said firmly. "I'm going with you."

## — Chapter 14 —

FORTUNATELY, Sam thought, as he was driving to get Hallie the next day after work, he was used to bossy females. In a household of four strong-willed women, he'd learned to compromise – not that he'd had much choice.

Perhaps "bossy" was too strong a term for this amateur sleuth he barely knew; "persistent" might be a better word, and she was definitely "curious."

To his surprise, Hallie was as prompt as he was, waiting by the front door of her home on Washington Street. Even though Cas had shown him her picture, he hadn't expected her to be so lovely. Long blonde hair, smooth pink skin, dainty nose, sparkling smile – she could be a movie star. He hoped her husband wasn't the jealous type.

"Cas just called from New York. He said to tell you hello and to try to keep me out of potholes," were her first words, as she climbed into his car.

"Potholes?"

"You know, traps? Danger? He's a worrier."

Sam was relieved; Cas knew where they were going and didn't mind. "He has reason to worry, from what I read about you online. You must be quite busy, helping the police and running a public relations business, too. How do you manage?"

"I work in my office from nine to five Monday through Friday, but people hire me for results. When they get results, I have time for my other interests. Also, I've a good staff, Cas travels a lot, and we don't have children – not yet, anyway."

"So many of these homes look alike," Hallie observed moments later, as they drove through the Marina district. "Are you sure you know the house?"

"It's the only one on the block with blue shutters. There, see it? I'd better grab this parking place."

"Anything about the house look different?" she asked, as they rang the bell.

Sam shrugged. "I wouldn't know. I was in such a hurry to escape."

Moments later, an older woman peered through the glass peephole, then opened the door. She wore what looked like a shower cap over frizzy white hair; her face was lined and unsmiling. "Yeah?"

"Sorry to disturb you," said Hallie, introducing herself and Dr. Butler. "We're trying to find a young woman named Polina Belnikov. We were told she lives here."

"That Russian girl?" The woman frowned. "We kicked her out."

"Mind if we ask why?" Sam inquired.

"She was supposed to be a housekeeper. She worked her ass off the first week, then we had to go away. When we came back, the house was a mess. Things were broken and missing. Why do you want her?"

"She borrowed a car from my friend," Sam answered, "and she hasn't returned it."

"Mercy me, I hope you catch the little thief!"

"We will." Hallie spoke with more confidence than she felt. "You have no idea where she went? Did she leave anything? Anything at all?"

"No, but I took a picture of her with my husband.

She sure knew how to shine up to him."

"Could we borrow the picture, Ms. — ?"

"Betty Davis. You can keep it for a hundred bucks."

"No way!" said Sam indignantly.

Hallie poked him with her elbow. "Fifty cash."

Betty Davis shrugged. "Okay."

Sam looked on speechless as Hallie took two twenties and a ten from her purse and handed them to the woman.

"Wait outside," she said, grabbing the money. "I'll slip the picture through the mail slot. I don't allow no strangers in the house."

"You're very wise," smiled Hallie.

Betty Davis shut and bolted the door. A minute later, the picture arrived in a faded envelope.

— Chapter 15 —

"*Mister* Betty Davis looks old and confused," Hallie noted, handing the photo to Sam. "I'll bet he has Alzheimer's and that's why his wife bolts the door – to keep him from wandering off."

"A logical assumption."

"Polina's quite appealing. Not many men would have turned her down."

"I wish you hadn't paid that old woman. I insist on paying you back."

"Not a chance, Sam. Do you think Betty Davis – or whatever her real name is – was telling the truth?"

He sighed. He'd learned not to argue with strong women. "I don't know. Olivia – my late wife – said I was too trusting. I tend to believe what people tell me. You don't think that's her real name?"

"No, I don't. I smell a rat – proverbial, that is. Wish I could sit in the car for the next few hours and see who goes in and out of that house, but I can't. I've a girlfriend coming for dinner."

"I understand. My stomach tells me it's that time, too."

"Say –" Her eyes lit up. "What about joining us? Margot's an opera singer. She's just out of a long-term relationship, and she's presently unattached, but I promise you your virtue will be safe."

He chuckled. "I know I'm old-fashioned about S-E-X, but I do believe it has to mean something. I've never been with anyone but Olivia, and never will be – unless I fall in love someday."

"You will, Sam, that's a given. We're just having lasagna – it's the only thing I know how to make – and salad. Won't you say yes?"

"Why, yes, thank you," he said, "I think I'd like that."

— Chapter 16 —

Margot Hellman was a petite woman who almost looked fragile – the last person you'd expect to be an opera singer, thought Sam, eyeing her across the room.

At first he'd found her cool and reserved, but as they chatted, she'd warmed up, especially when she talked about her profession. In turn, he'd related a funny incident with his worms. Her response had been hearty; her nose crinkled, her eyes narrowed, her whole body seemed to laugh along with her. He liked that.

At forty-six, she was eleven years older than Hallie, but they seemed to know each other well. Margot had never seen her friend's new house, and marveled at its lack of ostentation. Though the red brick façade was traditional, the interior reflected the owners' strong aversion to clutter.

A few fine paintings graced the walls, glass vases held fresh flowers, and the all-beige living room with its floor-to-ceiling marble fireplace and built-in bookcases seemed barely furnished – yet tasteful and welcoming.

The two guests followed their host into the breakfast room, and seated themselves at a round table.

"Sure I can't help?" Margot called to Hallie in the kitchen.

"No! Stay there and be nice to Sam."

"I *am* being nice, aren't I, Sam?"

"So far," he teased. "Tell me more about you. Did you grow up here? When did you start singing?"

She smiled. "I was born here. I always sang. As a child, I wanted to be like Doris Day – you know, tall, blonde, gorgeous. I had to settle for being short, dark, and plain."

"You're not plain at all." She wasn't "eye candy" like Carlie, but attractive in her own way. Deep blue saucer eyes looked right at you, straight brown hair with a strand that she kept brushing off her face, and a sweet, almost shy, dimpled smile made an appealing picture.

"When I was growing up, I had bands on my teeth, I was skinny, and I had nonstop eyebrows." She drew a finger across her forehead. "The boys used to tease me and say I misplaced my moustache."

She giggled. "Now I can laugh about it. My father died when I was little, and my mother loved opera. She'd bring home musicians who'd play piano and I'd sing along. I took voice lessons for years, got accepted to Stanford but decided to immerse myself in music instead – ushering at operas, concerts, taking courses. Then I got married. We lost our two-year-old daughter in a small plane crash, and our marriage fell apart – oh boy, that smells wonderful!"

Hallie entered the room bearing three plates and a tray of lasagna. "It's do-it-yourself time," she said. "In our house, every night is maid's night out."

"I'll just finish my saga," said Margot, as Hallie spooned the pasta onto colorful plates. "I was accepted into the Merola Program which grooms young soloists for the San Francisco Opera. After intense studying, I got the bad news. My voice wasn't big enough for the Opera House."

"You stopped singing?"

"I stopped singing grand opera. Now I teach music appreciation during the day and sing Gilbert & Sullivan at night, with a group called the Lamplighters. Oh, Hallie, this looks heavenly!"

The three ate and chatted till after ten, when Sam pleaded an early morning meeting. He thanked Hallie, promised to keep in touch, and turned to Margot. "Forgive me, but I have to ask – whatever happened to your misplaced moustache?"

She blushed. "My Mom took me to an electrologist when I was fourteen. It changed my whole life."

## Chapter 17

THE NEXT MORNING, Hallie couldn't wait to leave a message for Theodore "Teddy Bear" Baer, the overworked San Francisco Police Department detective she had helped solve a recent murder.

SFPD Lieutenant Helen Kaiser, Cas's former girlfriend, headed the homicide unit, and had assigned the officer to Hallie's case, warning her, "Everyone calls him 'TB.' Don't call him 'Teddy Bear' if you want to live."

An hour later TB returned Hallie's call. "No more bodies, I hope," he said tartly.

"Nope, TB, I just need a teeny favor."

He groaned. A stack of active cases faced him on his desk. A pushy socialite who dabbled in crime was the last person he needed. "What favor?"

"You know that computer program that scans a picture to see if it looks like somebody else?"

"I assume you mean Facial Recognitions technology, which matches photos to other photos in the criminal database."

"Exactly! May I give you a face to match?"

"Whose face is it?"

"Someone I'm curious about."

"Don't waste my time," he snapped. "What's going on?"

"Sorry, I was trying *not* to waste your time. It's a young woman, Polina Belnikov – B-E-L-N-I-K-O-V – who thinks the Russian mob is after her. She stole a car. I want to know if she has a record. Right now she seems to be missing."

"Has anyone made a police report?"

"Not that I know of."

"Well, suppose you bring yourself down to the station and fill out a stolen vehicle and a missing person's report. Do you have access to anything with her DNA or prints?"

"No."

Long sigh. "Fill out the forms, and we'll take it from there."

"Thanks, TB," she said, but he'd already hung up.

An hour later, TB called back.

"Hallie," he said, "I wrote down Polina Belnikov's name when you mentioned it. My new partner, Lenny, saw it on my pad and thought I wanted him to run it. Do you want to know what he found?"

"Yes!"

"Your 'Russian' girl has a sheet. Her real name is Polly Jane Hodges from Wichita, Kansas. Last year, she was picked up for prostitution, shoplifting, and a pair of DUI's. Her address in the Mission district was fake and her whereabouts are presently unknown. Does that help?"

"Immensely! Thanks, I owe you a lunch."

"Save it for your long-suffering husband," he said, clicking off.

— Chapter 18 —

THAT EVENING, Hallie dressed in her inconspicuous "stake-out clothes," borrowed Cas's old Volkswagen, and parked where she had full view of the house with the blue shutters.

After watching the front door for two hours, from seven to nine, she closed her notebook and drove home.

The next night, she dined with her brother, Rob Marsh, and his former-fashion-model wife, Darryl Woods Marsh. They lived nearby, thanks to Edith Marsh, who'd bought both of her children multi-million-dollar homes in Pacific Heights.

Nicknamed "Mumsy," because as Rob had once explained, "She's so *not* a Mumsy!" Edith Marsh was neither quaint nor cuddly. Tall and stately, with short, well-coiffed white hair, she was a handsome woman with a commanding presence.

Widow of the widely respected R. Stuart Marsh, former de Young Museum curator, art collector and connoisseur, she was also known to her children as the Queen of Control Freaks.

A strong willful person, indeed, Edith Doty Marsh had grown up on a cattle ranch in Montana, where she'd learned how to rope a steer, shear sheep, run a backhoe, and do almost everything the hired hands did. Watching a cow give birth had inspired her to want to become a veterinarian.

Zina and Pritchard Doty had encouraged their daughter's ambition. Their property covered 30,000 acres of fields and pastures, and they very much wanted Edith and her two sisters to live and rear their children on family land.

Pritchard Doty traced his ancestors back to the Mayflower – a fact he was not in the habit of keeping to himself. His frustration at having no sons to carry on the name was somewhat eased by the hope that his daughters and grandchildren would perpetuate his successful farming and cattle-breeding business.

Two-thirds of his wish came true. Edith's sisters married, and dutifully brought their two husbands back to the farm. Papa Doty built them homes on the property where they could live independently, but still work for the family.

Edith, alas, disappointed him. She fell in love with Bobby Marsh, an art history major she met at a party. When he proposed, she dropped out of veterinary school. They wed in 1970, and moved to Berkeley, California, where he had a teaching offer.

Sadly, the senior Dotys were never to know their West Coast grandchildren. Zina, Edith's mother, died in 1973, and her husband Pritchard succumbed to cancer a year later, leaving their assets, in equal amounts, to their three daughters.

Edith sold her shares to her sisters, ending up with a generous dowry. Her husband lost no time investing his wife's inheritance in as many French Impressionist paintings as $12 million would buy. After his death in 1998, the sale of a single Edouard Manet had allowed Edith "Mumsy" Marsh to become a generous benefactor of the arts.

Hallie had always taken Mumsy's domineering nature in stride, often giving in, then doing whatever she pleased. Not so her younger brother Rob, who resented his mother's well-meant attempts to involve him in art.

Music was his life, not some old paintings. In pursuit of a jazz guitarist career, he'd moved to Los Angeles, only to return home a few years later, discouraged, but not defeated. Fortunately, a generous trust fund allowed him to support his wife and six-month-old twin daughters, play his guitar, and live his American dream.

# — Chapter 19 —

DINNER AT HER BROTHER Rob's house was always a treat for Hallie, especially since Cas was away for the week and she didn't like eating alone. Darryl loved to cook, and once the babies were asleep, their nanny helped serve and clean up.

After a "truly decadent" chocolate dessert, Darryl excused herself to check on their identical twins, Coco and Mandy. Hallie and Rob remained at the table, chatting.

"No crimes to solve these days?" he asked.

"Strange you should mention that."

Seeing her face light up, he raised his palms towards her. "Hey, I was just making small talk. Whatever you're thinking the answer is no, no, a thousand times no!"

"You haven't even heard what it is. Now shush for a minute, Rob, and listen."

Ignoring his scathing look, Hallie continued, "A widower friend of Cas's, Sam Butler, met a pretty Russian gal, Polina, in his dance class. She's too young for him, but he gave her a ride home and she told him some tale about the Russian mob trying to kill her. When she didn't show up for the next class, Sam learned that she'd been seeing the dance instructor, had borrowed his car and disappeared."

"So who cares?"

"Well, I sort of got curious, so Sam and I went to the house where he'd taken her home, and this grumpy old lady said Polina didn't live there anymore. But something didn't feel right, so I checked with my police friend and learned that Polina's not the girl's real name. She's not even Russian. She's Polly Jane Hodges from Wichita, Kansas."

"So what?"

"So last night, I spent a few hours watching who went in and out of that house. There were two men – one looked young, maybe a college guy, wearing jeans and a ratty sweatshirt. He was there about forty-five minutes. Then along came this other man, dressed nicely. When the jeans came out, the suit went in. From the young guy's brisk walk and furtive glancing, I concluded that the grumpy old lady was running a whorehouse."

Rob rolled his eyes. "Why do you always jump to conclusions? Maybe she's an English tutor. Maybe an acupuncturist – or a psychologist. Maybe she reads palms."

"Nope, something unkosher's going on, and I need you to go there and find out what it is."

"You want me to go to what you think is a whorehouse?"

"All you have to do is ring the bell and ask for Polina. If the lady who calls herself Betty Davis says she's not there, just say you're a friend and does she know where you can find her. That's not so difficult, is it?"

He sighed. "When's Cas coming home? Why don't you send him?"

"He doesn't look the part."

"And I look like a guy who needs a whorehouse?"

"You look young and innocent – the blond hair and the freckles fool people. Please, Rob? Just take a quick run over and come right back."

"You want me to go *now*?"

"Sure, you're dressed perfectly in that old shirt and khakis."

46

"It's not old!"

She reached into her purse for keys, then scribbled on a pad. "Take Cas's Volkswagen. It's parked in front, and here's the address. It's the only house on the block with blue shutters. Darryl will still be upstairs with the twins by the time you get back."

"I must be crazy," he muttered, grabbing the keys and the paper. Then he headed for the door.

"Oh, and Rob, sweetie," she called out. "Try to look horny."

— Chapter 20 —

STILL GRUMBLING TO HIMSELF, Rob pulled the Volkswagen into a parking spot a few blocks away, and hurried toward the house with blue shutters. No lights were visible; with any luck, no one would be home.

To his disappointment, the lady who answered the door fit Hallie's description of Betty Davis, right down to the shower cap covering her frizzy white hair.

"Uh – hi," he said, trying to smile. "Is Polina in?"

"Who are you?"

"I'm a friend – uh, we have mutual friends."

"Polina don't live here no more. Go 'way," she said, about to slam the door.

"Wait," he said. "I have cash and I can pay."

She looked interested. "What's the password?"

"Uh – Polina?"

"Go 'way," she repeated.

"Okay, okay. Let me think for a second. Maybe I

should have asked for Polly Jane –"

"What'd you say?" She lit up.

"Polly Jane –"

"She *did* tell you the password." The door opened wide. "Come in, come in, young man. Rest your butt while you wait."

Cursing Hallie in his mind, Rob followed his host into the kind of living room he would have expected: shabby unmatched furniture shared space with velvet wall paintings and plastic orchids.

"Is Pol – Polly Jane home?" he asked, still standing.

"Yeah, just Polly – she don't like the 'Jane.' She's busy for half an hour. Then she'll see you. She tell you the rules?"

"If she did, I forgot."

"Cash only, payable in advance. A hundred bucks minimum, extras cost more. Over an hour, even a minute, it's another C-note. No refunds. Capeesh?"

"Yes, but unfortunately, I can't wait a half hour. Are there any other women –"

"Nope, just Polly. Ain't no one better!" She paused and eyed him suspiciously. "What's your name? You got an appointment?"

"My name's Tom. No appointment. Maybe I should phone her and make one."

"Polly don't talk to no one but me. I'll buzz her and see when she's free."

"That's okay, I –"

Betty Davis was already clicking her cell phone. After mumbling a few indistinct words, she waited for an answer, then ended quickly. "Polly don't know you, but she'll see you tomorrow at seven."

"Wonderful," he said, relieved. Then he held out a five-dollar bill. "Could I trouble you for a glass of water before I go?"

"Yeah, sure." She set the cell phone on a table and snatched the money. "Wait here."

A few minutes later, she was back with a paper cup of water. "Wanna pay now for tomorrow?"

"No." He drained the cup and hurried to the door. "Thanks for the drink. I'll let myself out."

"Bring cash."

A heavy click told him she had locked and bolted herself inside the house.

## — Chapter 21 —

HALLIE WAS RIGHT. Darryl was still upstairs with the twins when Rob walked in the front door, handed his sister her keys and said under his breath, "Never again!"

"What happened?" asked Hallie. "Are you okay? Did you see Polina?"

"I saw Betty Davis. And if I'd given her a hundred bucks and waited half an hour, I could have partied with Ms. Polly Hodges." He mimicked a high voice. "She doesn't like the 'Jane.' "

"Interesting – she's using her real name." Hallie walked into the living room and sank into a chair. "How sad, that a beautiful young woman has to sell herself to make a living. Were there any other working girls?"

"No, just Polly. I had to say I was coming back in order to get out of the damn place. Polly's expecting 'Tom' at seven tomorrow and I don't plan to be there. The ball's in your court now."

"Hmmm. I don't know brothel protocol. Can you phone and cancel?"

"Madam – and I do mean madam – Davis said that Polly doesn't take calls from anyone but her. So your clever spy – me, that is – offered her five bucks to fetch me a cup of water. When she went off to get it, I sneaked a peek at her cell phone and got the last number she called, which was Polly's. I wrote it down in the car. Here."

"Brilliant!" Hallie took the paper and jumped up to embrace him. "You're the dearest brother in the world. And you're getting to be a really great spy! Do I owe you five bucks?"

"Five thousand's more like it. What if someone had seen me there? What if the place had been raided? And what now? You call the police, they pick up Polly for hooking, the dance guy gets his car back and everyone lives happily ever after?"

"No," she said, "but don't worry about tomorrow, I'll take care of it. Let's go upstairs and watch Darryl watch the twins sleep."

"Yay," he smiled, "that's my kind of excitement."

## — Chapter 22 —

SAM BUTLER took Hallie's call Saturday morning and heard about Rob's adventure. Involving the police, Sam agreed, was not the answer. A repeat offender, Polly could be in for a long jail term.

Right or wrong, his instincts told him that she'd had a troubled childhood, little or no education, and had given up hope of getting a legitimate job. His three daughters had enjoyed all the advantages Polly never had, yet they, too, had experimented with sex, drugs and alcohol – that was today's world.

Fortunately, his girls had recovered and redirected their lives. Lina was the pre-school teacher wed to a doctor, Athena was a lawyer living with her gay partner in New York City, and the youngest, Jordan, worked in a wildlife orphanage in South Africa. If he could influence his daughters to change, maybe he could have some small effect on Polly.

Hallie explained that the phone number Rob had written down was useless. It rang and rang, and no one had answered. At one point, Sam suggested turning the whole matter over to Jeff, but he also realized that the dance instructor was furious with Polly, wanted his car back, and wouldn't hesitate to call the authorities.

"It's up to Jeff if he wants to report a stolen car," Hallie told Sam, "but you and I don't need to involve the police. You said you want to help the girl. Would you consider keeping 'Tom's' appointment this evening and try to talk some sense into her? I'll go with you and wait in the car.

Maybe you can find out what other skills she has, if any, and we can try to get her a decent job."

Sam thought hard. Should he duck out while he could, or listen to his conscience. Common sense told him not to get involved. The girl was trouble and he had nothing to gain by helping her.

Yet fate had thrust him in a position to help her. If he did keep the appointment, perhaps he could at least try to show her where she was heading. That wouldn't really be "getting involved," would it?

— Chapter 23 —

THAT EVENING, Hallie picked Sam up and drove him to the blue-shuttered house. When Betty Davis tried to slam the door in his face, he told her he was Tom's friend – that Tom had just been scouting for him to see if the place was safe. He recited the password, "Polly Jane", waved a bill, and as if by magic, the door opened. Ms. Davis showed him to the living room.

Shortly after seven, Polly appeared wearing a pink feathered negligee and too much makeup. Her seductive smile dissolved the moment she recognized her caller. "Why, hello, Sam Butler. Change your mind?"

The hoarseness in her voice startled him. "No, I haven't, Polly. But I paid for an hour of your time and I want my money's worth. Is there someplace we can talk – besides the bedroom?"

"Sure th – thing," she said, clearing her throat. "I'll just go grab some clothes."

"And I'll just go with you, because if I don't, you'll sneak out the back door." Athena, his middle daughter, had pulled that on him – twice!

She shrugged. "Have it your way."

He followed her up the stairs into a dimly-lit room. A large double bed took most of the space. Soft music played, and an unfamiliar scent filled the air. Probably cannabis, he thought, perching on the bed's edge. He watched Polly closely, aware that once she was dressed, she might still try to flee.

Her attempt to make light of the situation had little effect. After dropping her negligee, and making sure Sam saw what was underneath, she slipped off her stiletto pumps. "Know what they call these?" she asked, coughing loudly.

"Shoes," he said. "Are you all right?"

She nodded, pretending to wipe her nose, but spitting into the handkerchief. "They're CMF shoes."

"CMF?

"Come Fuck Me." She giggled, then pulled some clothes from a drawer. In minutes, she'd changed into a T-shirt, jeans and a pair of flip-flops. He insisted she leave the bathroom door open as she washed her hands.

"We'll have to talk here in the bedroom," she said, drying her fingers with a washcloth and plopping on the bed beside him, "or the old lady will listen in."

"I'll sit on the chair." He got up and moved across the floor.

She coughed again. "Why'd you come here, anyway? How'd you know my name?"

"Do you have a cold? A sore throat?"

"I'm fine. How'd you know my real name?"

"I'll tell you that if you answer my questions. Were you born in Wichita?"

"Sure. My mom was 14. She didn't know who my father was, and didn't want to see or hear of me again once she dumped me out."

"Were you adopted?"

"I should've been. But I was sickly – full of my mother's drugs – no one wanted me. So I went into the wonderful system (cough, cough). Lost my virginity at age ten to another foster kid." She reached into a drawer in the bedside table. "Mind if I smoke?"

"Are you crazy?" Jumping up, he snatched the pack of cigarettes. "Open your mouth!"

"Fuck you."

"Open your damn mouth or I'll do it for you!"

She opened and stuck out her tongue. He took a quick look and grabbed her arm. "You're full of sores and in-flammation. I'm taking you to the hospital."

"I won't go!"

"Then I'll take you to the police station."

"No – please! Who'll pay my hospital bills?"

"We'll worry about that later." Still holding onto her, he pulled her toward a closet and grabbed a coat. "Put this on. A friend named Hallie will drive us to St. Anne's. And forget the tears, Miss Polly Jane Hodges. They only work once."

# — Chapter 24 —
## *The Next Morning*

"YOUR FRIEND is quite ill, Ms. Marsh." The physician sighed deeply as he stood in the hallway of St. Anne's Hospital. "She's infected with oral human papillomavirus Type 16, a sexually transmitted virus. There are many strains of HPV but Type 16 is linked to oropharyngeal cancer. The good news is that Polly's cancer is mostly at the base of her tongue, an area that lacks pain fibers and often gets ignored till it's too late. But it responds well to conventional treatments – surgery, radiation, chemotherapy – and thanks to you, we've caught it early."

"Is she awake?"

"Yes. She put up quite a fight at first – insisted she wasn't sick and had to go home. I'm afraid we had to give her a shot to quiet her. But don't worry. Your friend is getting a thorough physical exam and workup, including toluidine blue staining to outline the biopsy sites, dental radiographs, MRI –"

"Sorry to interrupt, Doctor, but as I mentioned last night, Polly is not my friend. She's penniless, and she has no family to help out."

"What about the man who was with you last night – Mr. Butler?"

"He's at work today, and asked me to check on Polly. He met her in a dance class, and later learned that she was selling herself to stay alive. He has three daughters around her age and was concerned. But he's not a relative, he has no personal relationship with her, and no reason to pay her bills."

"In that case, I've good news for you. If she can realize how sick she is and agree to try a promising new treatment my research lab has been testing, we can take care of her expenses. We'll tell her all the pros and cons and she can either agree to our conditions, including a stay in rehab when she recovers, or I'm afraid we'll have to send her elsewhere."

"Is your experimental treatment safe?"

"Nothing is one hundred percent, but I'd use it on my own daughter. Briefly, we assess Polly's tumor cells looking for gene patterns to determine which drugs will best attack her cancer. We've had failures, but Polly's cancer is at an early stage, as I've said, so we'll know in a short time if our medications work. If not, we go to the tried and true."

"You mentioned rehab?"

"Polly's a pretty young woman. Once she's quit smoking and drugs, we want to be sure she stays clean. If so, we might ask her to do an education video for us. People think this is a rare cancer but it's actually epidemic. This year, in the U.S., 35,000 new cases of oral cancer will be diagnosed. The number keeps leaping, particularly among teenagers, who seem to think oral sex is safe. It isn't."

"Could she be giving the virus to men?"

"More likely, she got it *from* a man. Middle-aged men are at particular risk – white men in their fifties and younger. If you know someone she's been with, he needs to get checked for suspicious lumps in the neck, pain chewing, swallowing, or moving the tongue, bleeding sores, skin abnormalities, and so on. There's no reliable blood test to detect

HPV and it's serious business. Nature heals some patients, and some never get symptoms. Others, like Polly, ignore their symptoms. The cancer spreads to the lymph glands, and you know the rest."

Hallie nodded. "I do – and my friend Sam and I feel there's a good woman in there, under the makeup and foul language. If Polly can keep clean, she'll be a fine spokeswoman for you. Thanks, Doctor. I'll be back to see her later."

Polly was not in her bed when Hallie returned that evening. The nurse explained that she was in a conference room where the doctor and his colleagues were showing her a video about the new treatment and what could happen if she didn't treat her cancer. She finally agreed to try.

"That's good news," Hallie said. "Please tell her I've picked up her belongings and I'll keep them for her until she's released. And she'll be glad to know I've returned the car to its owner."

*PART 3*

## Chapter 25

LINA BUTLER HOLMES, Sam's oldest daughter, had warned her father that women were no longer afraid to be aggressive in social relationships. He'd replied that he could never be interested in a woman who took away his right to be the pursuer.

Carlie Gaines, often in his thoughts, was always friendly, even mildly flirtatious in dance class, though she'd made clear that she had no personal interest in him. Knowing she was involved with someone else, he tried not to respond, or even to think about her, yet he couldn't dismiss his feelings.

When his email contained an invitation from Margot Hellman to see Gilbert & Sullivan's *Pinafore*, however, he was thrilled. How flattering to know that at least one lovely woman wanted your company!

Tuesday evening, Sam showed up at the dance school shortly before five, and was quickly pulled aside by Jeff, the swing instructor.

"Thanks for getting my car back," he said. "I couldn't believe it when I looked out my window yesterday morning and there it was – parked right in front! How'd you find it? Some woman left me a note saying I should thank you for getting it back. Amazingly, it wasn't damaged, and I'm too busy to press charges – though I still think that crazy Russian broad should be behind bars."

"Sorry to tell you, Jeff, but she's not Russian, she's not crazy, and she's in the hospital with oral cancer." He lowered his voice. "Listen, if you've been – uh, intimate, you should see your doctor or dentist right away. You've been exposed to HPV-16, the human papillomavirus."

"That bitch gave me a disease?"

"Or vice versa. Have your mouth checked for sores, blisters or anything unusual."

"Jesus," he whispered. "That's all I need on top of everything else."

"What else?"

"Something's rotten in Denmark," he growled. "This school's going to hell. I'd swear someone stole a sweater out of my locker. And look at this beautiful maple floor! This is supposed to be waltz night and the janitor or someone spilled dance wax all over. Try it – lightly. And for God's sakes, don't fall on your ass."

Sam took a few steps and nodded. "It's slippery, but don't sweat it." He liked to use his newly-learned expressions. "Can't we tone it down?"

"With what?"

"I don't know – a wet mop?"

"Never use water on a waxed floor. Makes it worse."

"Sawdust?" asked Sam.

"I left my sack of sawdust at home."

They both started to laugh, just as a group of students walked in. After almost a month of lessons, Sam had gotten to know the eight women in the class, at least by sight. Carlie greeted Sam with an impersonal smile.

# — Chapter 26 —

As soon as the other students arrived, Jeff warned about the wax spill, adding that, "Anyone concerned about the floor is free to leave, and we'll credit you with two extra classes to make up for it."

No one budged. He went on, "A waltz generally needs a fast beat with plenty of twists and twirls, so tonight, let's play it safe and enjoy a slow rumba. Remember, it's relaxed and sexy. Carlie, c'mon up and we'll demonstrate. Good. Now take your partners' hands and listen to the beat."

He looked over at the couples, all females except for the two women lucky enough to corral the two males. "Be sure you know which one's the guy. The girl steps back, the guy steps forward. Okay now, girls: Backward, click, click. Forward, click, click. Too much hip action, Rhoda…"

Jeff liked to partner with Carlie, Sam noticed. She was a lithe, graceful dancer, thanks to her ballet training. He wondered – could Jeff be the man in her life?

He hoped not. The instructor was probably attractive to women in a smooth, slick way, strutting about in his body-hugging jumpsuit. His face was angular, his features stronger than he was, his hair dark, his suntan eternal. A seemingly unquenchable hunger for admiration made him seem vulnerable and strangely likable. And yet, Sam thought, Carlie deserved better.

A few minutes into the rumba, a sharp scream pierced the music. The dancers stopped abruptly, staring in shock. Mary, oldest in the class at sixty-two, lay on her back on the floor, crying and moaning. One leg was bent, the other lay straight, a small segment of bone protruding mid-calf. Sam dashed over and dropped down beside her. "Call 911!" he yelled. "Get an ambulance!"

Jeff was there in seconds, shouting into his cell phone. "They want to know what's wrong!"

"A broken leg!" Sam grabbed the victim's hand. "Hang in there, Mary. Looks like a fractured tibia. Help is coming."

"Y-you a doctor?" she gasped, between sobs.

"No, I'm a scientist. I know a little anatomy. Broken shin bones heal and rarely cause complications. It must be terribly painful, but you're going to be fine."

"Ohhhh, it hurts!"

Rhoda Starr-Stevens, a heavy-set woman loaded with jewelry came running over. She thrust a rolled-up towel at Sam. "Put it under her neck. Heavens, this is all my fault. I talked her into taking this class. Oh, Mary, I'm so sorry!"

"It's not your fault." Sam lifted Mary's head gently, slid in the towel. "Please, everybody, stand back. Jeff, for God's sake, class is over. Send your students home!"

— Chapter 27 —

As THE ROOM QUICKLY EMPTIED, Sam stayed by Mary, smoothing her brow, trying to keep her calm. When help arrived, Rhoda joined Mary in the ambulance, and they drove off, siren blasting. Half an hour later, Rhoda called Sam's cell phone to report that Mary was in surgery.

Jeff seemed so upset, Sam stayed to help him clean the blood and try to sweep up some of the wax.

"What bothers me most," sighed Jeff, scraping away at the floor, "is that Mary told me she has that awful bone disease —"

"Osteoporosis."

"Yeah, and that her bones could break easily. She said her doctor told her she needed low-impact exercise, and she wanted to know if this class would be okay. I said sure, as long as she took it easy and didn't try the fancy stuff. I should've known better."

"Nonsense. Don't blame yourself. Just find the idiot who spilled the dance wax."

Sam assured Jeff that Mary didn't seem like the type to sue, and if she did, the school undoubtedly had insurance. Then, confident there was little more he could do, he set down his broom and went home.

*PART 4*

# — Chapter 28 —

ON A SUNDAY MORNING in early April, happy to have mailed his taxes a day earlier, Sam sat relaxing in his library, a small book-lined room where Olivia used to write her poems. With a sigh, he thought about how much he missed his beloved wife, then remembered her advice about getting out and mixing with people. She'd be happy to see him now.

Her last words, and his promise to honor them, had somehow emboldened him to face the world's realities. And though his daughter Lina had made very clear that she and her sisters feared people would take advantage of him, he'd proven – to himself at least – that he was far stronger and more self-reliant than his daughters thought.

The new Sam Butler, in fact, had finally emerged from his cocoon…from the comfortable mental cave he'd shared with his worms for thirty-plus years, safe from the trials and trivia of everyday life.

He was even beginning to like this strangely challenging world. He hadn't expected to get involved in the dance class crisis, yet both the instructor and his students had stood there, too scared and dazed to act. Taking charge of a stressful situation had come naturally.

He'd also surprised himself by insisting on dragging Polly, a young woman he hardly knew, to the Emergency Room. Much to his relief, Hallie had been so upset at Polly's constant coughing when they drove her to the hospital, she'd taken over as her "advocate."

The latest news, Hallie had related, was that Polly had been released from the hospital to a halfway house. When the disappointed doctors realized their experiment, part of a series of clinical trials, had failed, they sent her back to the hospital for surgery. Polly was now undergoing chemo and seeing a speech pathologist to help restore her voice.

Having visited her twice in the interim, Hallie had found her upbeat, grateful, and determined to turn her life around.

Mary hadn't fared as well. Her leg, still in a cast, was healing, but dancing school was out forever. Rhoda Starr-Stevens had stayed on.

Instructor Jeff, addicted to gossip, had confided to Sam that the wealthy widow in her fifties was "hooking up" with the "salsa prick" in his thirties.

"She was probably a pretty blonde once," he'd added. "Those big blue eyes still gaze adoringly at every male she meets. But she's had so much plastic surgery – facelift, cheek implants, lip injections – she can barely smile. And her tight face doesn't match her flabby arms. Women over fifty should never go sleeveless."

Fernando Ruiz, on the other hand, was a magnet to the opposite sex. One of four dance instructors at the school, the dark-skinned Argentinian excelled in charming and flattering the ladies. He stood about five-foot-ten, a head taller than Rhoda, and as Jeff reluctantly admitted, "The man dances superbly, despite being a pompous asshole who wears tight pants and pads his crotch."

Sam had spotted Fernando strutting about the school, and one time, Jeff had introduced them. Fernando's deep brown eyes, Sam remembered, were focused and intense, his teeth either false or newly whitened, and his nose twisted slightly to one side – the result, Fernando was quick to explain, of a wooden plank that fell on his head while he was rescuing a child in an earthquake.

"Yeah, sure," Jeff had said later. "No one believes that bullshit except Rhoda. She's not only paying top dollar for dance lessons, she also treated the schmuck to a South American cruise."

"Do I hear a touch of jealousy?"

"Are you kidding? Do you realize what he had to do to earn his fare?"

"I guess he thought it was worth it," Sam said, with a grin.

If only Olivia could see him now, he mused. His naiveté was melting faster than an ice cube in a microwave.

— Chapter 29 —

HOME ALONE most of his spare time, Sam was beginning to enjoy introspection – an activity he'd long avoided. Aware that his ability to be objective was questionable, he nevertheless found himself an intriguing study. Stranger still, he discovered he liked himself. The more he thought about "taking over" in stressful situations, the more he realized it wasn't really a new facet of his personality.

When he'd learned that his daughter Lina was sexually active at fourteen, it was he, not his strait-laced wife, who'd taken her to get fitted for a diaphragm. And when her sister Athena announced that she was gay and Olivia cried all night, it was he who convinced his wife that Athena had been born that way and had every right to choose her own mate, whoever he or she might be.

He recalled, too, that when Jordan, their youngest, had drug and alcohol problems, and Olivia shrugged, "Oh, she'll get over it," he was the one who signed her into rehab and made sure she stayed till she was good and clean.

Maybe his people skills were lacking, and maybe he had no idea of the price of tomatoes, but he'd been a caring, conscientious father for many years. Now that he was out there living in the real world…Sam Butler could damn well take care of himself.

— Chapter 30 —

A CALL that Sunday evening reminded Sam that he had a date with an intriguing young woman – at least forty-six *seemed* young, and the few gray streaks in Margot's hair assured him she didn't mind growing older. He'd bought a DVD of *Pinafore*, and after watching it twice, pronounced himself an instant fan.

"Then you're a Savoyard," said Margot. "The Savoy Theater in London was built for Gilbert & Sullivan operettas, and the fans became known as Savoyards."

"Glad to know there's a name for us." He chuckled. "I've even ordered *The Mikado* and *The Pirates of Penitence*."

"*Penzance*."

"Yes, well, whatever. Margot, please forgive me, I'm new at this dating game and you're my first real date. I should've called you instead of waiting for you to call me, and I apologize. Should I – er, may I take you to dinner before the show?"

"That's lovely of you, Sam, but I'm actually in the show. I have to be at the theater early for costumes, makeup and all that. I'll leave your ticket at Will Call, and perhaps we can get something afterwards. I never eat before I sing."

"Where will I meet you?"

"The Lamplighters – that's the name of our company – have a custom. When the performance ends, all the actors come out in costume and meet the guests, so I'll see you there, then make a quick change and rejoin you in the lobby. Remember, it's this Saturday, April sixteenth, at eight o'clock. You won't forget, will you?"

"I'm counting the days," he surprised himself by saying.

— Chapter 31 —

THE NIGHT OF THE SHOW, Sam discovered that Margot had also invited Hallie and Cas, who were seated next to him. At intermission, they all raved about Margot's performance as "Little Buttercup," and the professionalism of the talented actors.

"Gilbert and Sullivan love to lampoon snobbery," noted Cas.

Hallie nodded. "Their tongues are firmly planted in their cheeks. Imagine naming a warship *Pinafore*, after a little girl's lacy apron! The costumes, the sets, even the dancing is satirical. Speaking of same, how's your dance class going?"

Sam shrugged. "Strange things keep happening."

"Like what?"

"Oh, like stuff missing from lockers, stopped up toilets, 'accidents' like spilled dance wax that caused a woman to break her leg, graffiti on the outside wall…and it's all happening at once. If I didn't know better, I'd think we have a malevolent ghost."

"Have you reported this?" asked Hallie.

"The owner, Tobias Miller, called the police. They came, looked everywhere, took lots of notes, and he hasn't heard from them since."

"Hmmm – methinks I smell a story," said Cas. "Could I send a reporter to sniff around?"

"You'd have to check with Tobias. I doubt he'd want the negative publicity."

"I've a better idea," said Hallie, as a buzzer ended the intermission. "Maybe Cas and I should take some dance lessons."

Sam stayed late that night, sitting in Margot's living room, sipping wine, and chatting about everything. It was almost one a.m. when he apologized for keeping her up so long, and offered his hand. Instead, she stood on tiptoes, kissed his cheek, and thanked him for a wonderful evening.

Embarrassed, he turned and walked quickly to the elevator.

— Chapter 32 —

THE FOLLOWING TUESDAY, Hallie asked Sam if he'd mind picking her up on his way to dance class. He was delighted.

"Cas sends his best," smiled Hallie, settling into Sam's front seat. "Said he needs dance lessons like he needs another wife. It's just as well. I snoop better alone."

"In that case, please be subtle. I don't want my dance-mates to think I'm bringing a spy."

"I'm there strictly to audit the class and see if I want to sign up."

"Excellent! And watch out for Jeff, the instructor. He hits on – is that the term? – anything female under seventy."

She waved her gold wedding band. "I just say I'm married to a wrestler."

The class was going well. Jeff did notice Hallie's ring, sensed Sam's possessive demeanor, and came to the wrong conclusion: So what if she was married. Sam *had* to be bonking her. It didn't stop the instructor from inviting her for a dance.

Sam looked on with amusement, then approached Jeff as the music ended. "Where's Carlie?"

"She's sick. I talked to her Sunday and she felt awful. Said she'd eaten at some offbeat restaurant and has food poisoning. She sounded terrible. I told her to call a doctor."

"Did she?"

"I don't know. I called twice today and left messages. She didn't call back. That's not like Carlie."

Sam frowned. "I've gotten to know her a little, too – strictly as a father figure. I hope she's all right." He paused a quick second, then added, "I'll stop by on my way home."

— Chapter 33 —

THE DANCING continued until Jeff announced a short recess. Chattering voices were interrupted by the sudden appearance of the salsa teacher, Fernando Ruiz. "Sorry to disturb," he said in an agitated voice, "but I mees my watch! *Con permiso,* anyone has seen my gold watch?"

Rhoda Starr-Stevens hurried up to him. "What happened, Fernando?

"*Cara,*" he said, kissing her cheek. "I always take off beautiful watch you geev me before class, lock in my locker, so no one steal. Today, I look – and I look – and I look more, and *Dios mio*! No watch!"

"I'm sure you've just misplaced it," said Rhoda, both embarrassed and pleased by his familiarity. "Can we talk later?"

"*Si, si, querida mia,*" he answered, not wanting to offend her. "Sorry to bother. I look in my car." And off he went.

After class, Hallie was bursting with questions. Sam filled her in on what was already obvious: yes, the socially prominent Rhoda Starr-Stevens, who wore so much jewelry columnist George Christy once called her "a human chandelier," and the poor-but-sexy Argentine Tango King were an item – of sorts.

Four first class instructors (and their assistants) worked at the school, Sam explained. Brigitte specialized in traditional dance and the Viennese Waltz, Jennifer taught Hip-Hop, Wobble, and Funk (street) dance, Jeff led the swing, jazz, and freestyle class, and Fernando covered the Latin beat. But according to Jeff, Fernando was always screaming that Jeff was broaching on his territory teaching rumba, samba, and Zumba.

"I'll teach whatever I damn please," were Jeff's exact words, "and Fernando can go screw himself." They were not friends.

Hallie learned that like Rhoda, Carlie Gaines, whom she had yet to meet, came from wealth. She lived in an elegant condo on Russian Hill and had told Sam that she was looking for a new career. Her social life centered around half a dozen men, one of whom she planned to marry.

Jeff had no idea which restaurant had served the suspected food, nor who was with Carlie at the time. He was sure, however, that she wouldn't have gone to an "offbeat restaurant" alone.

Sam offered to drop Hallie at home before he went to check on Carlie, but as expected, his offer was refused.

## — Chapter 34 —

PULLING INTO the driveway of an impressive-looking high-rise on a steep Taylor Street hill, Sam rolled down his window and poked out his head. A doorman materialized instantly.

"We're friends of Ms. Gaines," Sam announced.

"Is she expecting you?"

"No," said Hallie, leaning forward. "Her dance teacher has been trying to call her for three days and we're worried. Perhaps you can take us to her apartment so we can make sure she's all right."

"Wait here, please."

The doorman took a few steps, reached for his cell phone, then held it to his ear. "No one's answering," he said. "Could I see your I.D.?"

Sam produced his drivers' license; Hallie flashed a "Deputy Police" card Cas had gotten her from his ex-girlfriend, SFPD Lieutenant Helen Kaiser.

"Thanks, Mr. Butler," said the doorman. "You and the lady can park in the garage, leave your keys, and meet me in the lobby."

An oversize globe with dangling crystals shone down on the indoor entrance to the building. Louis XIV-style chairs, potted ferns and marble floors conveyed a sense of quiet luxury.

As Hallie and Sam walked in, a tall, dark-suited African-American man was waiting. He held out his hand. "Blair, Security."

Introductions, handshakes, then Hallie explained their mission.

"I understand your concern, Ms. Marsh, but Ms. Gaines often leaves town without notifying us."

"She would've told her dance teacher," protested Hallie. "He's tried several times to reach her and no one answers. He said she was quite ill the last time he talked to her."

"When was that?"

"A few days ago."

"In that case, let's check it out."

— Chapter 35 —

THE ELEVATOR rose swiftly to the nineteenth floor. Blair led the way down the hall to a door. He knocked several times, rang the bell and called out. No response.

As soon as his master key turned in the lock, they entered the spacious apartment. A sour smell greeted them. "Stay here," ordered Blair.

Hallie ignored the command; Sam followed her.

The living room and kitchen were clear. Then Blair opened a door down the hall. Hallie peeked over his shoulder and uttered a cry. A woman lay face down on the bathroom floor, her head half-buried in a puddle of watery vomit. Blair rushed over, tried for a neck pulse, then frowned. "It's Ms. Gaines. She's gone."

Sam controlled his shock as he reached for his phone. "Get back! Don't touch anything! That smell isn't decomp, it's something else – possibly toxic. Yes – hello? 911? We have a cadaver and a bad chemical smell. Call the coroner or the CDC. Yes, we'll wait. Yes, send the hazmat crew. No, we won't move the body."

"CDC?" asked Blair.

"Centers for Disease Control and Prevention. If food or drink killed Carlie, we have to find the source before anyone else gets sick. It could be staph, salmonella, E. coli – from that smell, it could even be some sort of biohazard. Whatever it is, we have to know as soon as possible!"

## — Chapter 36 —

AS SAM TRIED to calm his nerves, and Blair sought to analyze the situation, Hallie excused herself "to find a bathroom." A few steps down the hall, she turned a knob to what she hoped was the bedroom, but saw only a small office. An iPad sat atop a pile of papers on a cluttered desk.

Farther down, she opened another door and quickly

closed it behind her. A stronger smell enveloped her as she faced a large double bed, unmade, and stained with more vomit.

Knowing she had only minutes, she slipped on the gloves she always carried, searched the tables on both sides of the bed, then spotted a large dresser. Instinctively, she opened the second drawer, the one most women use for lingerie, tossed the bras and panties, found nothing. A glance into the spaces below yielded only sweaters, scarves and handbags. What was she looking for? She had no idea.

The closet was her last hope of finding some sort of clue. A variety of hats sat neatly arranged on a shelf, including a pointed cap with a strange bulge. Reaching up inside, she pulled down a bag of…clown makeup! Damn! She had only seconds to put it back before she heard the knob turning.

"I thought this might be a bathroom," she heard herself explaining.

Blair wasn't fooled. "Good thing you brought gloves, Ms. Marsh. Mr. Butler told me you like to solve mysteries."

"Umm – well, yes. But I do need…to go over there." She crossed the room to a half-open door leading to a bathroom, and locked herself inside.

Losing no time, she peered into the medicine cabinet over the sink: low-dose aspirin, birth control pills, antihistamines, and a collection of health supplements and vitamins. Nothing seemed unusual.

On the top shelf, however, a folded white napkin caught her eye; it was wrapped around a small black book. Glancing at her watch, she grabbed the book, dropped it into her purse, flushed the toilet, ran the sink water, and emerged.

"Anything in the bathroom?" asked Blair.

"Just me," she smiled. "Have a look yourself."

— Chapter 37 —

IT TOOK THIRTY MINUTES for a three-man-team from the coroner's Hazardous Material & Mobile Decomp Unit to arrive. Wearing oxygen masks attached to back-hoses, white Teflon suits with steel-toed boots, heavy rubber gloves, and carrying mops, buckets, and other equipment, they immediately closed the bathroom door behind them.

Forty-five minutes later, the team leader emerged, reporting that they had taken pictures, cleaned and neutralized the body, mopped the floor and taped off the bathroom. Samples of rug, towel, and curtains were bagged. The cadaver was sealed separately.

Hallie stopped one of the technicians who was wheeling out the body bag on a gurney. "Pardon me, do you know time of death?"

"Yeah," he answered, "we can usually figure TOD within a two to four hour window. Judging by body temp and lividity, we're guessing she's been dead about twelve hours. We'll know more when the coroner gets the liver temperature."

Hallie uttered a groan. It all seemed so impersonal. Next stop would be the lab at the morgue where they would dissect her body, examine her organs, and learn what they could. Medical science was a business, like any other. Once you're dead, you become a "thing."

Assured by Blair that the building manager would

notify whoever was important in Carlie Gaines's short life, she and a teary Sam left the scene.

## — Chapter 38 —

MINUTES LATER, Sam parked in front of Hallie's house. Walking her to the door, he apologized for his strong reaction, and regretted having subjected her to such a traumatic discovery.

"It's curious," said Hallie. "I never met Carlie, as you know, but finding her like that was horrible. Any thoughts about what happened?"

Sam hesitated. "Carlie was jitterbugging all over the place at the last lesson. We had dinner not long ago, and she was a happy, vibrant woman who was deeply involved with someone. She wouldn't say who he was, but it doesn't matter much now. As to what killed her, I have no idea. It looks like it might be some sort of poison."

"Food poisoning?"

"I checked online while you were chatting with the technician. Three thousand Americans die from food poisoning every year; I wouldn't rule it out. I can't imagine anyone wanting to hurt Carlie, everyone liked her. But if you think there might be some other cause of death, maybe you should talk to her lawyer, the one she's been dating. I suppose it's possible she had enemies."

"The thought occurred to me. On a different subject, what about Fernando, the salsa guy? Do you think someone stole his watch?"

"Who knows? As I told you, Hallie, strange things

keep happening at that school. We've got more than 200 students – maybe one's a kleptomaniac."

"Or a sicko. By the way, I hope you don't mind if I sign up to join your class. I really *should* perfect my two-step."

Once inside the house, Hallie found Cas stuffing his suitcase for a late night plane trip. She kissed the back of his neck, and hurried upstairs to her office. As soon as she sat down at her desk, she took out the small black book – and realized it was locked.

After ten minutes of struggling with various keys and a screwdriver, she begged help from Cas. Knowing that a car was en route to pick him up, he restrained his impulse to ask questions, opened a drawer, took out a short billy club he kept for emergencies, and broke the lock with a single hit.

"Thanks, wonderful Mr. Fixit," she said. "Is there anything you can't do?"

"Yes," he said, returning to his packing, "keep my wife out of trouble. Will you at least *try* to behave while I'm gone?"

— Chapter 39 —

CARLIE GAINES – a woman Hallie had never known. She paused as she prepared to open the dead woman's possession. Had she the right to read something so personal? A quick review of what she knew about Carlie raced through her brain.

"High maintenance," Sam had said, when asked about their relationship. "Too pretty, too flirty, and too

79

young for me – unfortunately."

Forty was also way too young to die. Online photos showed Carlie at various social events – always in expensive clothes and jewelry, stylized hair, and a warm, half-innocent smile. Sometimes she was pictured with attractive men, never the same one.

Sam had told Hallie about Carlie's parents' divorce, Carlie's failed careers, and her late mother's bequest which supported an indulgent lifestyle. But still, Hallie wondered, what kind of a woman was Carlie Gaines?

— Chapter 40 —

THE LITTLE BLACK BOOK turned out to be a challenge. Carlie had used it both as calendar and diary, with comments in a private code.

Her dates, for instance, were identified by a one letter initial, occasionally followed by a number under ten. After a few minutes of study, and judging by mentions of breakfast, Hallie guessed that "J – 3" meant that Jim (Joe, Jack, James?) was not much of a lover, whereas "N – 10" meant that Ned (Nick, Norman, Nelson?) was hot stuff.

Hallie knew she could be totally off base, but it was a start. And "N" seemed to be someone Carlie saw quite often. Doctors' and dentists' appointments were written out clearly, as were hair dates, massages, manicures, pedicures, dressmaker fittings, luncheons, meetings, and all other engagements, including her dinner with Sam. No number followed Sam's name.

At the back of the book, an A-Z section listed what

appeared to be frequently used phone numbers as well as addresses. Among them, she found Carlie's lawyer, Nate Garchik – of course! He was the sizzling "N" in her diary. His cell phone was listed with the notation: "Pvt – don't give out."

An emergency was different, however, and social etiquette allowed one to make calls up to nine p.m. With eight minutes to go, she dialed quickly.

A man answered.

"Mr. Garchik? I'm Hallie Marsh. Sorry it's so late. I'm calling you about Carlie Gaines."

"Marsh," he repeated. "You related to Edith Marsh?"

"My mother."

"Remarkable woman. We sit on a board together. You're a friend of Carlie's?"

"Not really," she answered. "Could I come see you for a few minutes?"

"I'm due in court first thing in the morning. Is there a problem?"

"Yes. I have some bad news. I don't like telling you on the phone."

"I'm quite busy."

The message communicated. "All right. I'm sorry to tell you that Carlie died this morning. A friend of hers from dance class and I found her body."

A moment's silence, then he asked, "Is this some sort of joke?"

"I don't joke about things like that, Mr. Garchik."

"Oh, my God!" he exclaimed. "Hold on, I – I have to sit down. What happened? Was she hurt? Are you sure?

Was there an accident?"

"No accident. We don't yet know the cause of death. According to Jeff, her dance instructor, she was suffering from food poisoning. He'd been calling her for the last few days, but she never called back. My friend, Sam Butler –"

"Yes, yes, the worm guy. Carlie liked him."

"They were good friends. Sam brought me to the dance class. I often work with the police, so when we heard Carlie didn't answer any of Jeff's messages, Sam and I offered to stop by her condo."

"Oh, my God," he repeated softly, as the news began to register. "Where did – how was – did she suffer?"

"We won't know till we hear from the coroner. If she was poisoned by something she ate in a restaurant, they have to take action right away."

"Yes – that – makes sense." He sounded numb.

"Please accept my condolences, Mr. Garchik. I'm told you were good friends."

"Friends?" His voice dropped so low she could hardly hear him. "We were getting married. She wanted to tell her other suitors in person, then we were going to announce it. I have a jeweler designing our wedding rings."

"Oh, dear, I didn't know. I'm terribly sorry! Sam had heard Carlie say she was seeing her lawyer, so I thought I'd better notify you right away. The security guard at the condo said they'd inform her family."

"Family? That lunatic father?" His voice rose an octave. "If they let Herb Gaines into her condo, he'll rip off everything in sight!"

"Forgive my asking, but doesn't Carlie's will –"

"Carlie doesn't have a will! We were in the process of setting up a revocable trust. She hated her father. He's a no-good parasite. She wanted to leave her money to St. Anthony's Foundation, to feed the poor."

"Not even an old will?"

"She died intestate." He sighed. "Carlie was a hopeless procrastinator. I adored her but sometimes she drove me crazy. I shouldn't be telling you all this."

"Does attorney-client privilege apply after she's dead?"

"Yes, unless I can get a waiver. Damn it, Ms. Marsh, I –"

"Hallie."

"All right, Hallie. The last thing Carlie would want would be to have her estate go to her father. I'd better get right on it. My partner can represent me in court tomorrow. I need more details. Can you come to my house right now?"

"I'll be there in ten minutes."

— Chapter 41 —

NATE GARCHIK, short in stature, deep in voice, greeted Hallie at the door. A neatly-trimmed gray moustache and beard made him look older than his fifty-plus years. About five-foot-eight in height, he stood square, trim, and muscular. Beads of perspiration dotted his forehead. Struggling to control his voice, he uttered a shaky "Hello."

The moment he spoke, Hallie felt a strong sense of masculinity, confirmed by the solid, almost painful squeeze of his handshake. Handsome he wasn't, but he didn't need to be. His sex appeal was clear and unmistakable. Hallie recalled that if he were the "N" in Carlie's black book, he was also the "10" for prowess in the sack. It was all coming together.

A tiny monogram on the pocket of his shirt and a shiny "H" on his belt buckle indicated expensive tastes. Worn-out sneakers showed a dedication to exercise, but his face was drawn and pale as he focused on his visitor. "I should have known something was wrong. She usually texts me back right away. I've been so damn busy…"

"May I come in?"

"Oh, sorry. Please do." He led the way into a living room filled with knickknacks, photos, trophies, travel souvenirs. The furniture had simple, straight lines, the coffee table was covered with magazines and newspapers, and a tall totem pole stood guard over a grand piano. "Please – sit down. What happened?"

She paused a few seconds, then sank onto a couch. "The security guard let Sam Butler and me into her apartment," she began. "We found Carlie on the floor of one of her bathrooms. Jeff, the dance teacher, said he'd talked to her recently and that she'd complained of food poisoning. Sam's a former medical student and thought that might be the COD – cause of death. But we have to wait for the coroner's report."

Nate nodded sadly. "We were working on her will. She was very casual about such matters. She didn't like to deal with what she called 'icky' subjects. And yet, she was adamant about having an up-to-date Advance Directive – a living will. She saw her mother die a long, agonizing death, and didn't want to suffer the same fate."

The lawyer wiped his eyes. "Saturday night, we went to this South of Market restaurant a friend recommended. We ate the same food – it was delicious – and I didn't get sick."

"Exactly the same?"

"Yes, goulash for both of us. No desserts. She had a lot of allergies. Maybe she was allergic to something. Sunday we were going on a picnic, but she phoned that she was feeling ill and would call me later. When I didn't hear back, I sent several texts urging her to see a doctor. She texted back once, saying she'd talked to her doctor. He wanted to make a house call, but she said it was nothing, she'd be fine in a day or two. And now – now – I can't believe she's gone…"

— Chapter 42 —

THE ROOM was silent a few minutes. Then Hallie spoke softly. "Nate," she said, "It's none of my business, but the apartment had a strange chemical smell. Since you both had the same food at the restaurant – might there be another cause of death?"

"You mean suicide? Never! She didn't do drugs. She hated taking pills. She was big on health and nutrition. Her body was almost sacred to her."

"Did Carlie have any enemies? Rejected suitors who might want to harm her?"

"You mean *murder*? Good Lord, no! Everyone adored Carlie, she was a people-magnet. Even her discarded boyfriends loved her."

"Do you have names?"

"No. I was often busy evenings, and encouraged her to go out with others, so long as they were just friends. She talked a lot about Sam, said he was the father figure she never had. And she mentioned her dance instructor – Jim?"

"Jeff."

"That's it. He was interested in taking their dating to the next step but she said he was a dork, to use her word. She mentioned that Latin guy, too."

"Fernando?"

"Yep, add him to the list of would-be lovers."

He paused a few seconds, shook his head, then went on, "Carlie had no children or siblings. Her parents were divorced. Her mother died some years ago and left her a small fortune. Her dad's still alive, last she heard from him. Herb Gaines was always broke, always after her for money. Not only that, he served prison time for fraud and embezzlement. You said someone was notifying her family?"

"Yes."

"Then you can bet the old man's on his way here. He used to send her desperate emails. Too bad we don't have Carlie's iPad. She emailed Gaines in no uncertain terms that she was writing a will and leaving him out. I advised her not to do that, but I know she did. That would at least prove her intent."

Hallie perked up. "Couldn't we get the iPad? I doubt that the apartment's officially a crime scene."

"I have a key. She wanted me to move in with her. I wanted her to move in with me. She was dying – oh, bad word – she was anxious to be my interior designer – oh,

Lordy! She still has my daughter's Louis XIII Fortuny pillows she borrowed for a photo shoot. They're worth a bundle."

"Maybe you should pick them up before her father gets here. Do you know the doorman?"

"I know all the doormen. Even that tight-ass Blair. I'll go get the pillows, but I can't very well walk out with her iPad."

"You could hide it between the pillows." Hallie reached into her purse for a card. "Call me when you get home? Even if it's late?"

"Will do," he said, walking her to the door.

## — Chapter 43 —

IT WAS AFTER eleven when Nate called. "The place stinks," he told Hallie. "We left the windows open to let the rooms air out. Blair let me in to get my pillows and stayed glued to me every second; I couldn't even look around. I did manage to poke my head in her office. Funny, her iPad was gone. It always sat right on her desk."

"It was gone?"

"Gone."

"How strange," she murmured. "It was there earlier, just after eight. Could someone have taken it between the time we left and the time you got there? But how could anyone get into the apartment with those two bloodhounds, Blair and the doorman, guarding it?"

"Damned if I know, Hallie. I'm exhausted, but I'm going to my office. I'll be working all night. Got a pencil?"

"Yes."

He rattled off a number. "That's my direct line. Call if you hear or think of anything."

— Chapter 44 —

NO SOONER had she clicked off the phone, than Hallie dialed the night doorman at Carlie's building. Alex Moore was instantly defensive. He'd come on duty at eight p.m., just as the men were removing the body, and no one but the lawyer had been up to Ms. Gaine's apartment since then.

Hallie sensed his uneasiness. Blair had shadowed her and Sam around the apartment as if he were guarding the Hope Diamond. The security chief was much too uptight to bend the rules. It had to be the doorman.

"Look, Alex," she said to him, "if you're lying, and we find out about it, you'll not only lose your job, you'll be disgraced and go to jail for obstructing justice. On the other hand, if you tell the truth now, and it leads us to Carlie's iPad, which is missing, you'll be a hero. No one needs to know the details."

A long silence was followed by a weak voice. "It wasn't my idea –"

"Just tell me what happened, Alex. No lies."

"Uhh – God help me! Okay. This sharp-looking dude wearing a hat and dark glasses comes by a little after nine, says he's Carlie's brother. Shows me his picture ID: Richard Gaines. Says he's working on a project with Carlie and needs to get into her place right away. I say no, Blair told me not to let anybody in, but the dude won't take no. Then he says that if I can just get Carlie's iPad for him – he describes it to me – I won't have to let him in."

"Go on," said Hallie.

Long exhale. "I still say no, and the guy takes out some bills. Says he can make ten grand on this project if he gets the machine in time, and he'll give me a grand just to get him the friggin' thing."

"Yes?"

"That's a lotta bread for me, I gotta feed my family."

"Go on."

"So at that point, I figure it's okay, he's her brother. I wait till Blair goes off duty, then I run up, get the damn thing and stash it in the bushes. The dude said he'll come back at three a.m. to pick it up and bring me the cash. That's all I know."

Hallie took a long breath. "Listen carefully, Alex. Carlie had no brother. The man's a phony. But I've an idea. I'm coming over to get the iPad right now. I'll return it to you long before three."

"Hey, what if her brother comes early?"

"I told you, she had no brother! I'll have it back to you in an hour, long before the man's due. When he comes, don't tell him anything. Hand him what he wants, take the money, and I'll videotape everything – his face, his car, the license..."

"What if –"

"No what-ifs! I'll be by in twenty minutes."

# — Chapter 45 —

SHORTLY before midnight, Hallie picked up the iPad and drove to the impressive Montgomery Street offices of Garchik, Dooley & Bechtle. Nate was waiting for her. He only needed five minutes to copy Carlie's files.

Hallie returned the machine to Alex by one a.m., thinking how lucky she was that Cas was on his way to Washington. He would never have let her get involved in a stranger's death, much less be out alone that late.

Checking her watch, she spread a small blanket on the ground, behind a bush in the front garden. Alex had his instructions, and she had a clear view of the almost-hidden iPad. Her camera was at the ready; light from the street lamp would suffice. All she had to do was settle there, shivering in the night air, and try to stay awake for two hours.

Sometime before three, a noise broke her reverie. A car drove up to the entrance. Within seconds, Alex emerged from the lobby and approached the vehicle.

Hallie sat up, ears perked, camera ready. Suddenly, she stopped in alarm. While she'd been dozing, the night fog had crept in, obscuring her view. The car door opened and a figure stepped out, barely visible in the thick mist.

Attempts to take pictures would be useless. "Damn!" she said to herself. Alex and the stranger moved closer to her, and began arguing. The stranger was demanding "the goods." Alex wanted to see the cash.

Only a few yards away, she watched as Alex led the man towards her hiding spot, then stopped, spread the branches of a nearby bush, and retrieved the iPad.

"I'll take it," she heard the man say, in a whiny, nasal voice.

"Where's my money?" asked Alex.

"I've got it – right here." Reaching into his pocket, the man drew out a gun. Panicked, Hallie rattled the branches around her.

"Who's there?" the man yelled, twisting toward the noise. Hallie ducked down, giving Alex time to reach for his own gun. The man was quicker. A sharp kick to the groin made Alex cry out, drop his weapon and double over. The man grabbed the iPad, dashed to his car and drove off.

Hallie ran to the spot where Alex lay curled on the ground, clutching himself. "Take deep breaths," she ordered. "I'm calling an ambulance."

"No! Please!" Alex looked up and forced a smile. "I'll be okay. The son-of-a-bitch got away! You get his license?"

"Nope. No pictures, either. Too foggy."

"Was he going to shoot me?"

"He sure as hell wasn't going to pay you."

Alex groaned. "If you hadn't been here, I'd be dead."

"Probably." She was relieved to see he finally let go of his crotch, and was trying to get up. "Here. Take my hand."

He struggled to his feet. "Thanks." A long sigh. "What happens now? Do I lose my job?"

"No. Relax. Chances are, Blair won't even notice that the iPad's gone. Just go about your work as usual. If anyone questions the missing machine, tell the truth: you told me about the phony brother and we set up a sting. You were going to make the sale, then hold the man while I called the police, but he drew a gun and escaped. That's the truth, and I'll back you up."

"Got it," he said, starting to move away.

"Alex," she called after him, "have you learned anything tonight?"

"Yeah," he answered, limping toward the lobby. "Don't trust nobody!"

— Chapter 46 —
*Wednesday*
*five hours later*

THE PHONE woke Hallie shortly after eight a.m. Explaining that he only had minutes to spare, Nate listened to her story of the iPad fiasco, scolded her for placing herself in danger, then spoke fast. "I'm off to see a judge who owes me a favor – we'll freeze Carlie's assets right away, put her property in storage, close her bank accounts. I think I can convince the judge that she was writing a will and leaving Herb Gaines the grand sum of one dollar. The bastard may be in town by now. He'll try to dissipate her assets as soon as he can."

"You'd better get moving."

"I've notified the banks not to release anything to anybody, and warned the building manager not to let anyone in – especially her father. No question he hired the guy to steal her iPad. If he tries to alter the emails, we've got the originals, thanks to you."

"That might take some explaining. Stolen evidence isn't admissible."

"Right, but his evidence is stolen, too. And we have

two eye witnesses, you and Alex. One never knows what a guy like Gaines might try to pull. Our copy of Carlie's emails is insurance against his trying to alter them. Don't forget to report the theft to the police."

"I was hoping we wouldn't have to."

"Are you serious? You were involved in the commission of a crime. Just leave out the part about bringing the iPad to me to copy. By the way, I spoke to the coroner, Dr. Toy. Told him it was a probable homicide, so he'll give the case priority. He's – oops, sorry, gotta take this call."

## — Chapter 47 —

AN HOUR LATER, Hallie phoned Dr. Thomas Toy, the forensic pathologist she had worked with before. After the usual questioning by an aide, he came on the line.

"Haven't heard from you in a while, Hallie," he said almost cheerfully. "Which body interests you?"

"Would you believe me if I said I just wanted to say hello?"

"No. It must be Ms. Gaines. You always pick my most difficult cases."

"You're a mind reader, Dr. Toy. I know how busy you are, but – was anything obvious? Were there any bruises?"

"We only got the body last night." He spoke patiently. "If you remember, Hallie, the first thing we do is try to determine time of death, exact cause, and what, if anything, preceded the death. In this case, there were no outward signs of a struggle, no external injuries."

"That doesn't eliminate the possibility of murder."

"No, it doesn't. If you recall, we take biological specimens from the deceased for toxicological testing, including stomach contents. In this case, we expect to find one or more 'poisons,' i.e. chemicals. We have to take extreme care. Postmortem deterioration along with the gravitational pooling of bodily fluids could cloud the results."

"And?"

"When that happens, the toxicology tests may overestimate the quantity of the suspected chemical and give us false answers. Say – I'm glad you called, Hallie. Did you know Ms. Gaines?"

"No, but I've talked to her friends and I know where you're going. Carlie was a happy person with everything to live for, including a fiancé. He said she didn't do drugs, hated to take pills. No one who knew her thinks it could have been suicide."

"I thought so. Vomiting one's insides is a most unpleasant way to die. No one would choose to suffer that way."

"Oh, dear, that poor girl. What happens now?"

"Testing will take time. Do you know if she's been to any foreign countries recently?"

"No, but I'll find out."

"That would be helpful. Leave a message with any information you can get, even if it seems trivial. Then call me in three weeks."

She knew better than to ask for a rush job. "Thanks, as always, Dr. Toy."

# — Chapter 48 —

DRESSING quickly, Hallie drove to the Central Police Station on Vallejo Street and asked to see her "friend," the over-worked homicide detective, "TB" Baer.

After sending word he had to finish his paper work, he emerged twenty minutes later, and greeted her with a forced smile. "What now, Hallie?"

He was even taller than she remembered, towering over six feet. She recognized the same ruddy complexion, the nose that looked as if it had been flattened in a bar fight, his strong voice and sturdy handshake. The smile hadn't fooled her the first time they met, and it didn't fool her now. His eyes were steely cold. They seemed to penetrate her thoughts.

"I know you're busy. I won't stay long." Noting that he didn't invite her into his office, she told him briefly of Carlie's questionable death, then explained that, "Alex, the night doorman, was visited by a man pretending to be her brother. He tried to bribe Alex to steal her iPad, so we planned a sting to catch him."

"You did what? Are you crazy? Why the hell didn't you call us?"

"The man sounded like a pro. I was afraid he'd spot a stakeout car. Right after the sale, Alex was going to arrest him, hold him, and then call you."

TB frowned. "You'll never learn…"

"Anyway, the guy showed up around three this morning, pulled a gun, grabbed the iPad and drove off without paying."

"Serves you right. Did you get a look at him? Catch a plate?"

"Unfortunately, no. Too much fog."

"What about Alex?" He sounded exasperated. "Can he give us a description?"

"It happened so fast. All I could see was that the man was white, about five-ten, maybe in his fifties. He wore a light-colored fedora with a black band. Dark glasses, dark clothes, dark hair, I think. He kept his head down. Had an unpleasant, whiny voice."

"Let's see now. You've got yourself a dead woman, but you don't know if she died by her own hand or by foul play. She's got a father she hated who's about to claim her estate. A white guy in dark glasses steals her iPad. And how you got yourself mixed up in this mess is more than I care to know."

He paused to calm himself. "If it proves to be a homicide, we'll investigate. Otherwise –"

"But they're pretty sure –"

"Hallie," he said, striving for control, "there's nothing I can do until we hear from the coroner. If you want, you can go to the front desk and file a report about last night. It will show that you acted foolishly and improperly, used poor judgment, broke several laws, endangered yourself and a citizen, and that your story has more holes than a shooting range. Why don't you just go home and make babies like other women do?"

He shook his head, groaned, "Why do I even bother?" and walked away.

Disheartened by both Nate and TB's scolding, Hallie drove

home, reminding herself that she hadn't had much sleep. A quick call to Ken Skurman, her trusted assistant, reassured her that the office was doing fine; no immediate crises. Tossing her clothes on a chair, she fell into bed and didn't open her eyes till late afternoon.

*PART 5*

— Chapter 49 —
*A Week Later*

CARLIE GAINES' Memorial Service at Grace Cathedral was well-attended by friends, acquaintances, ex and would-be lovers, many of whom had known or worked with her in her various stages of evolution.

A tearful Nate Garchik, describing Carlie as "the only woman I ever loved," gave an emotional eulogy. Yet sadly, as Hallie noted, there was no fire in his voice. The reality of her death had drained his dreams. He seemed sad and subdued, almost a different man.

After the Wednesday morning service, Nate reported that in the absence of a will, the court had appointed him Administrator of the Decedent's Estate, and granted his request to freeze her possessions. Her jewelry, personal belongings and furniture were in storage until he could get them appraised. For the moment, all her assets were untouchable.

Nate was relieved that he'd won that round, but Hallie's instincts were right; grief had dulled his anger. There were moments when he was tempted to say, "The hell with it!" and let her father take all. But for Carlie's sake, he knew he had to fight.

He'd never met Herb Gaines, and didn't see anyone at the funeral who looked like Carlie's picture of him. Typical of the creep, he guessed, not to show up at his daughter's funeral.

Herb Gaines, however, was definitely in town. His fast-talking lady lawyer, who called herself "Sloane," was apparently reluctant to go to court with a stolen iPad for evidence and a convicted felon for a client. She was calling Nate daily, pressing him to sit down and discuss a "reasonable" settlement.

Nate kept stalling. If Carlie's death proved to be accidental, he might be willing to pay off her father and get on with his life. If the coroner's report showed that she was poisoned, however, he wouldn't have to look far for a suspect.

— Chapter 50 —

CAS had often observed that his wife wasn't happy unless she was plotting something – and usually, he noted, it was something unnecessary, illegal, or dangerous. In this instance, however, he was a willing accomplice to her matchmaking.

Their friend Margot, the opera singer, had had a single date with Sam Butler, the night she performed in *Pinafore*. Margot reported they'd had a wonderful chat after the show, and she'd been certain Sam would ask for another date – but he hadn't.

Hallie had explained that he was new at the dating game, and suggested the old ruse: call him, say a friend gave her two tickets to something, and invite him. Margot declined, explaining that she had too much pride.

So Hallie stepped in, as she often did. Sam had once mentioned his love for Impressionist art, and she'd promised him a visit to Mumsy's house. After getting Margot's okay, Hallie phoned her mother, who'd been delighted to hear from her busy daughter. Hallie and Cas wanted to come to dinner and bring two friends, Margot and Sam.

Sam was thrilled to accept the invitation, and pleased to hear that Margot would be there. The stage was set for Sunday, the first of May.

— Chapter 51 —

ON THE DOT OF SIX, Hallie, Cas, and Margot arrived at the Marsh mansion on outer Broadway, San Francisco's "Gold Coast." Designed in 1920 by famed architect Willis Polk, the handsome Georgian manor boasted four stories of red brick respectability.

Spanning two lots, the structure had views in almost every room, an indoor swimming pool with a retractable ceiling, a three-car garage and a well-manicured English garden.

Margot's eyes widened as Grimaldi, the longtime family butler, led the guests down a thickly-carpeted hall to the living room. Having been warned that their host was a collector of just about everything, Margot marveled at the difference between Hallie's ultra-minimalist decor, bereft of "clutter," and the Marsh mansion, where every available space was filled with antiques, art objects, and paintings. But oh, those paintings!

Sam arrived moments later. He caught up with the group, air-kissed Hallie and Margot, just as Olivia had taught him, shook hands with Cas, then began to notice his surroundings. Coming face to face with a Degas on the wall, only steps away, made him gasp aloud.

He was, in fact, noticeably moved as he met Edith Marsh and took a seat on the couch next to Hallie. Grimaldi had given the guests a brief tour, pointing out a Monet haystack painting, a Cézanne and a Sisley, even a full-length Renoir.

What do you say to a woman who owns some of the world's greatest masterpieces, he wondered. "Nice collection"?

"That magnificent Renoir…" he managed to blurt, "seems a bit at odds with the typical Impressionist plein-air paintings."

Edith Marsh was used to stunned visitors. "That's a fine observation, Dr. Butler. And did you notice the Belle Epoque attire?"

"Indeed," he said excitedly. "Renoir's subjects are almost always fashion-conscious. Perhaps that modern element keeps him labeled an Impressionist rather than a traditionalist."

"True. The Impressionists were pioneers. As you know, they refused to study at the French Academy and broke new ground." Not wanting to bore the other guests, Edith turned to Margot. "Speaking of talented artists, I understand you sing opera."

Margot was delighted to take the spotlight. Conversation flowed as the guests sipped champagne and began to relax. The host mentioned that although she had a box at the Opera House, her children had only used it twice last year. Cas promised they would do better. Since the advent of subtitles, he said, he'd actually begun to enjoy grand opera.

"Don't get excited, Mumsy," warned Hallie. "He liked *Carmen* but he'd never last through *Tristan*."

## Chapter 52

A SHORT TIME LATER, at the dinner table, Hallie addressed her mother. "As you know, Sam's a molecular gerontologist at the Buck Institute. I didn't mention that he works with worms. Tell us, Dr. Butler, what do you do with the squirmy creatures?"

Sam's face lit up. "I'd put you all to sleep if I gave details. But I can tell you that we try to identify agents that extend lifespan and prevent age-related diseases such as Alzheimer's and Parkinson's. We work with worms, extremely simple organisms, the most elemental of beings."

"What have you discovered?" asked Cas.

"We've found factors that lengthen the life of these worms. For instance, certain stressors – say several hours of exposure to higher temperatures – enable the creatures to live up to thirty percent longer than their unheated peers. We hope to apply findings like that to human cell cultures…um, I'd better stop there."

"Fascinating!" said Edith. "When can we expect results?"

"We've made exciting discoveries, Mrs. Marsh. So far, however, the Fountain of Youth has eluded us."

Always happy to score points with his mother-in-law, Cas said, "You're a long way from looking or acting old, Edith. Don't you agree, Margot?"

"Most certainly! I was expecting…"

As she rambled, Sam seized the chance to whisper to Hallie, "Any news?"

"Awaiting the autopsy report," she replied in a low

voice. "The coroner can't identify the COD."

"What are you two whispering about?" demanded the host.

"A dead body, Mother. Aren't you sorry you asked?"

"Whose dead body?"

Sam quickly answered: "We were concerned about the COD – er, cause of death of a mutual friend, Mrs. Marsh. We stopped to look in on her the other evening, and sadly, found her dead. It was puzzling because I'd never seen a body with such strange-colored skin."

"What color was it?"

Hallie sighed with relief. Sam had succeeded in stirring Mumsy's interest before she could deplore her daughter's attraction to corpses. But what was he talking about?

"Her skin was pale blue. I had two years in medical school," Sam continued, "and I saw a great many cadavers. There's the dark blue-purplish color of cyanosis, when the blood lacks oxygen, and there's a reddish-blue skin reaction to certain pesticides. This was a light blue tint I'd never seen before. Even stranger, it only lasted minutes."

"You never told me that," said Hallie.

Sam smiled. "You saw the back of her head, then ran off to search the house. But I saw Carlie's neck when I felt for a pulse. It was definitely blue. By the time the body was removed, the color was gone."

"Did you tell anyone?"

"I told one of the hazmat guys. I'm not sure he believed me."

Edith Marsh cleared her throat loudly as Grimaldi

appeared, followed by a maid in a black uniform. Both were carrying individual soup bowls.

"My favorite!" said Hallie, quick to change the subject. "Our chef, Lucas, makes the most orgasmic cream of asparagus soup."

Margot stifled a giggle, then asked, "What about you, Hallie? What's happening in the PR world?"

"Omigod, *everything*! Have you heard of the Internet? Facebook? Twitter? The whole process of communicating with the public has been reborn. Cas is thinking of doing a feature on it – aren't you, darling?"

Sensing her desire to get away from worms and corpses, he began expounding on the fate of the newspaper industry.

His wife sent a wink of gratitude.

## — Chapter 53 —

FROM HALLIE'S point of view, the dinner was a success. Sam drove Margot home, and as she reported to Hallie the next morning. "He asked if I'd spend the weekend with him in the wine country. I said I'd love to. Then he assured me that we'd have separate bedrooms. Damn men! Don't they know that a woman's yes means yes?"

Hallie laughed. "He's delightfully naïve in some ways."

"I'm not so sure. He seemed quite taken with your mother."

"He was taken with her art."

"I know. How can I compete with Renoir?"

"You don't have to. Mumsy has a beau, Stewart Woods, my brother's father-in-law. He's been very devoted, although he couldn't be there last night. He manages to keep Mumsy guessing. But don't worry, Sam will come around. Have patience."

Ignoring her own advice, Hallie couldn't wait to call Dr. Toy. "I know it's only been a week and a half," she said excitedly, "but I have new information. How goes the investigation?"

"Slowly," he replied. "When the COD is undetermined, the state requires us to videotape the autopsy. As you can imagine, that takes extra care and time. But at least we've eliminated staph infection, E. coli, listeria, salmonella – now we're testing for less common poisons."

"Have you eliminated food poisoning as the cause of death?"

"If you mean food from the restaurant, yes. What's your news?"

"My friend Sam, who was with me when we found Carlie, told me that – well, she was face down, so all he could see was the back of her neck. He said it was pale blue when we got there, and an hour or so later, when your hazmat team arrived, it wasn't blue anymore."

The medical examiner paused. "That suggests a type of poison I hadn't thought of. Did you find out if she'd been to any foreign lands?"

"Yes, her fiancé said she was in Brazil about five years ago, but she hadn't left the country recently."

"Brazil – hmm. I'll do a blood smear and test for

Chagas. She may have been infected by a parasite. With this disease, the victim has no symptoms for years, then suddenly it becomes acute and fatal."

"Sounds terrible."

"It's a guess, but worth checking. Another few weeks and I hope to have some answers."

*PART 6*

## — Chapter 54 —

HALLIE HAD NO CHOICE but to be patient – a virtue, she acknowledged, that she often lacked. After marking "May 25 - call Dr. Toy" on her calendar, she phoned Nate Garchik. His office in the financial district was not far from hers; could she come by and get an update? He agreed to see her at three that afternoon.

Garchik, Dooley & Bechtle was luxurious in every aspect; fine art works, sweeping windows looking out on panoramas of the city, ultra-modern décor. Recalling her brief midnight visit, she marveled at how much better everything looked in the daylight. A toothy blonde receptionist sent Hallie down the hall.

Nate Garchik came out from behind a cluttered desk, and greeted his visitor with a smile.

Hallie gave him a quick hug. "You're looking better than the last time I saw you."

"Thanks," he said, "Have a seat. I'm feeling better. But this guy Gaines is a piece of work."

"Tell me."

"His lawyer, Sloane, still phones every day." Nate sank into a high-backed chair. "I rarely take her calls, but when I do, she gets very pushy. She didn't like hearing we had a copy of Carlie's email telling her father that she was disowning him, and denied any knowledge of the iPad theft. I've got her on tape telling me I can't use stolen evidence, but if she didn't know about the theft, how did she know the iPad was stolen?"

"Good question."

"I've told her I need to see Gaines in the flesh. She claims she doesn't know how to reach him. Says Gaines drops into her office now and then or calls from a disposable phone."

"BS."

"Pure BS! I told her I'm not taking any more of her calls till I meet with Gaines. I've begun the probate process. The court lets me decide who gets what. I told her if Gaines wants to make any claim to her estate he'd better get his ass in here PDQ."

Nate went on to explain that he assigned one of his aides to get appraisals on Carlie's belongings, and to see if the St. Anthony Foundation needed furniture. At some point, he said, he might even be willing to settle with Gaines in order to get closure.

Hallie suggested they wait until they hear from Dr. Toy. The unspoken question was on both their minds. What if Carlie's death was no accident?

— Chapter 55 —

FOR THE MOMENT, the case was on hold. Hallie used the time to catch up on her PR commitments, Sam and Margot continued their platonic dating, Nate buried himself in work, and problems at the Dancing School stopped as suddenly as they had started.

About four weeks later, on the first day of June, Hallie got the long-awaited call from Dr. Toy.

"We've completed our examination of the evidence," the coroner said. "As you know, I had to assign the body a manner of death: Natural, Accident, Homicide, Suicide, or Undetermined. Since Ms. Gaines was soon to get married and seemingly had everything to live for, I eliminated the possibility of suicide. People who try to commit suicide don't call in sick to their doctors."

"I agree."

"There's little doubt that Ms. Gaines died from kidney failure due to some virulent poison. The manner of death convinced me it was not accidental. In short, we have uncovered enough evidence to believe that a crime was committed. I had to rule it a homicide."

"Wow – thanks, Dr. Toy. What do we know about the poison?"

"The honest answer is not much. We've narrowed it down and eliminated all the obvious and even some of the most obscure poisons. At one point, we were sure it was ricin. She had all the symptoms: slow onset, nausea, vomiting, diarrhea, respiratory distress, pulmonary edema – but the urine test for the presence of ricinine was negative. So we're still looking."

"I guess that'll have to do for now. You'll send autopsy reports to her lawyer and the police?"

"They've been notified. Good luck finding a killer."

— Chapter 56 —

THE CORONER'S determination was positive in one sense. It meant that TB would have to keep his promise. Hallie remembered the detective's exact words: "If it proves to be a homicide, we'll investigate."

111

The tall, burly policeman was not surprised to get a visitor that afternoon. "Damn it, stay out of this, Hallie," were his first words, as he met her in the hall of the police station. "Let us do our job. There's a killer out there and I don't need another corpse."

"I've no intention of being one – not yet, anyway."

"Remember that! All I can tell you is that I spoke with Mr. Garchik this morning. He needs to see the victim's father, Mr. Gaines, but Gaines' lawyer insists she doesn't know how to reach the old man. She gave us a description and we sent out a bolo – an all-points bulletin."

"I know what a bolo is," Hallie snapped, annoyed at his condescension. "It stands for 'Be-On-the-LOokout' for so-and-so. Why is her father so important?"

"Who else would profit from her death? Unfortunately, we have no *legitimate* proof that Carlie wanted to disinherit him."

Hallie ignored his not-too-subtle reference to the iPad caper. "Have you run her financials?"

"She was quite conservative. Her money was tied up in Munis, CD's, and the S&P 500. We did find a recent withdrawal of twenty-five thousand dollars. That's all I can tell you. Now will you please go home?"

"No, I plan to stick around and bug you all day."

"Very funny," he said, pointing with his finger. "There's the exit."

— Chapter 57 —

AN HOUR LATER, Hallie was back in her office when the cell

phone rang. Seeing "SF Police Department" on her caller I.D., she wondered if it was TB, phoning to apologize for his rudeness. Or maybe he was worried that she might complain to his supervisor.

"It's Inspector Baer," he said, when she answered. As if she didn't know that gravelly voice. "I think we may have picked up the man who stole Carlie Gaines' iPad. You told me you saw and heard him that night. I need you to come in and make an ID."

"I caught a quick glance of him in the dark – In a thick fog. I couldn't possibly pick him out of a lineup."

"No lineup. You said he was wearing a fedora. That's what made me suspicious. He's still wearing the damn thing, won't take it off. Would you recognize the hat? The voice?"

"Umm – maybe." She wasn't about to blow the chance to find out what was going on. Nor was she going to mention that Alex, the night doorman, had seen him more clearly.

"You can stand outside the interrogation room and look in. Can you be here in half an hour?"

"I'll have to hustle, but yes, I can be there."

"Good," he said, and clicked off.


— Chapter 58 —


IT TOOK about five seconds for Hallie to recognize the voice and hat of the man who called himself Freddy Fedora.

Seated at a table opposite TB, the man spoke in short sentences, obviously intoxicated at four in the afternoon, but still coherent. The black-banded fedora he wore was exactly as she remembered, and his high-pitched nasal tone unmistakable.

Staring through the one-way window with TB's partner, Lenny, and their Supervisor, Police Lieutenant Helen Kaiser, she noticed that Freddy Fedora was thin, with a deeply wrinkled face and a long nose. He was surprisingly well-dressed in a beige turtleneck and brown sports coat.

"I see that your real name is Bernard Rothheimer," TB began, casually adjusting his earpiece so Lieutenant Kaiser could relay questions. "You've quite a sheet – fraud, petty larceny, boosting cars, domestic abuse –"

"Yeah, li'l wifey was a bitch. Hooked up with anything in pants – or should I say *out* of pants, ha ha…"

TB frowned. "You were arrested in a bar fight less than an hour ago. Suppose you tell me what happened."

"Yeah, sure, why not. This dude owes me for a job. He tries to stiff me. I punch him. He punches me. The bartender breaks us up and calls the cops. End of story."

"You laid hands on him first?"

"He asked for it."

"What kind of job?"

"It don't matter. We had a deal. He fucked up."

TB glared in mock anger. "You're wasting my time, Bernard. I might as well throw you in the drunk tank and come back tomorrow."

"Hey, man, no! The name's Freddy and I ain't goin' in no drunk tank. What would you'd done if some asshole screwed you out of a grand?"

TB flinched. He was old-fashioned enough to wish Hallie weren't listening. "We've got you for disturbing the

114

peace and obstructing justice. I can hold you for a week, Freddy babe, and the big boys down there are going to love you to pieces."

"Hey wait, man, you can't do that!"

"Talk to me, Freddy."

"We got a deal? I talk, I can go?"

"Depends what you tell me. What's the name of the man you punched?"

"Herb somethin'. Met him in the bar a few months ago."

TB thrust a composite sketch across the table. "Is this the man?"

"That's the bastard! Got any water?"

"In a minute. You say you met Herb a few months ago. Where?"

"Same damn bar."

"This is important, Freddy." TB's tone relaxed. He was starting to get answers and Lieutenant Kaiser was shooting questions into his earpiece. "Can you give me a better date?"

"Hmmm – yeah. We were hittin' the booze pretty heavy. The creep shows me a roll of bills. Says someone – he ain't sayin' who – gave him twenty-five grand. I say let's go to the bank to make sure the bills are OK. He says it's some freakin' holiday, somethin' about Presidents, and the banks are closed. So he gives me a big one, ya know, a hundred smackers, says it's a down payment, and the bartender says it's good. So I'm thinkin' he's a dude to know, get my drift? Hey, guy, I'm dyin' of thirst."

"OK, Freddy. While I'm getting your water, think

about the rest of your story. If you start to get creative, I'm tossing you in the tank."

## — Chapter 59 —

"THAT'S THE MAN," said Hallie, as TB closed the interrogation room door and stepped outside. "No question."

"Appreciate your help," said the detective. "We're grateful for your time, but we won't be needing you anymore."

Hallie looked to Helen Kaiser in alarm. "Can't I stay?"

"It's against – "

"It's okay, TB. She may have something to add."

He started to say, "She can also be a pain in the butt," then thought better of it. Rumor had it that Hallie's journalist husband used to hook up with the pretty Lieutenant. "Okay, boss, sure. Get him some water, Lenny?"

"I do have something to add," said Hallie. "I thought you were brilliant to get that date out of Freddy, TB. I just checked my iPhone. Presidents' Day was February 21st. Carlie died on April 19th. That means her father was here – living here – at least a few months before she was murdered."

"Exactly!" TB beamed. Compliments were rare in his profession. "We have a strong suspect, a solid motive, and now we know that Gaines had plenty of time to plan his daughter's death. The only question is how he did it. Want to sit in, Lenny?"

"Yup. Here's your Hetch Hetchy."

The detective took the glass from his partner, and turned the door handle. "Let's go see Dr. Einstein."

116

## — Chapter 60 —

"HERB AND ME, we was buddies," explained Freddy Fedora, as TB handed him the water and sat down. Lenny preferred to stand.

"The old guy told me he's goin' on seventy, his back was killin' him, so he moved here from –?"

"France."

"Yeah, that's it, France. Said he's got a rich daughter here."

"Go on."

"So I see him every night at this bar. Finally he cops out that he went to see his kid in this swanky apartment, and she gave him twenty-five grand to stay away from her – forever. Cool, huh?"

"He agreed?"

"Yeah, said he needed the dough. He didn't sign nothin' but she tells him it's on her computer, in case he tries to get funny."

"What's on her computer?"

"Like I said – that she paid him off to stay away from her and never ask for nothin' more."

"Herb Gaines was okay with that?"

"Yeah, until she kicked the bucket. Herb said he ain't had nothin' to do with her gettin' whacked, but I ain't so sure."

TB stared accusingly. "Maybe he had help from a friend? A drinking buddy."

"Hell, no, man, I didn't smoke the bitch. But Herb, he says screw the agreement, he's her only relative and he should get her dough. He hires me to get the computer thing so there ain't no record that he got paid off. Capeesh?"

"Perfectly. You stole the iPad – it wasn't a computer. Did you give it to your friend Herb?"

"Yeah, sure, I take it right to him at the bar. Says he's real glad to get it. Says his dough is tied up at the moment but I'll get me my nine big ones soon."

Freddy emptied the water glass, then wiped his mouth with his hand. "That was right after he learned his daughter croaked. After that, he don't come to the bar no more, and I find out he ain't livin' at his hotel. So I'm thinkin' he skipped out on me."

TB glanced at his watch. "And today?"

"So today, weeks and weeks later, I go to the same bar where we met, I get myself a beer and a ham sandwich and who walks in but the shithead himself. I go up to him and demand my dough. He says the computer thing ain't no good to him cause his daughter's lawyer has a copy of what's on it. Says he already gave me a hundred smackers and he ain't gonna pay me no more for somethin' he can't use."

"That's when you punched him."

"Yeah."

"Who's got the iPad now?"

"How the fuck would I know?"

"Okay." TB clicked off his tape recorder. "Herb Gaines, the guy you punched, isn't here to press charges, Freddy, so you're free to go. Here's my card. If you see Herb again, I expect you to call me, day or night. And if I see that damn fedora at this station again, I'm throwing the book at you. Capeesh?"

"Yeah, yeah, man. I'm outa here!"

Late that afternoon, Hallie dutifully reported the scene to Nate, wondering why Carlie hadn't asked him to write up a legal agreement with her father. Nate explained that Carlie never mentioned that her father was in town.

*PART 7*

## Chapter 61

Two days later, on a Friday, Sam picked Hallie up a few minutes early for their five o'clock class. He'd gotten a call from Tobias Miller, the dance school owner, to stop by his office and to bring Hallie, if possible. She'd met Tobias when she signed up for the class, but hadn't spoken to him since.

Tobias seemed pleased to see her, and greeted Sam like a longtime friend. "Thanks for coming, both of you," he said, gesturing to a pair of chairs. "I know you're trying to help the police find out what happened to Carlie, and so am I. A reporter from the *Chronicle* was here asking a lot of questions – who her friends were, and so on. I'm wondering if I should have told him that Carlie was interested in buying the school."

Hallie's eyes widened. "You're selling the school?"

"I've been thinking about it. I'm almost sixty, I've worked hard all my life, and it's time I married my girlfriend – we've been together seven years. I'd like to enjoy life a bit."

"Good for you!" Sam smiled approvingly.

"Who else knows about your plans?" Possibilities flooded Hallie's mind.

"All my staff know but I told them not to tell anyone. I've no idea how Carlie found out. I wanted the instructors to have first crack at it, just as I did. You may not know this, Hallie, but I started out as a dance teacher here. When the school was up for sale, I was lucky enough to get some investors to help me buy it. When I could afford it, I bought them out."

"And you've made it a huge success. Have any of your

instructors seemed interested?"

"They all have. But I'm not sure any of them have the means. Maybe they'll partner up."

"Carlie could have afforded it," Sam observed.

Tobias nodded. "She seemed quite interested. Said she was going to talk to her lawyer, her accountant and some other people. I thought this might possibly have some bearing on your investigation."

"Did you tell the police?" asked Hallie.

"No. That big tall guy – "

"TB."

"Detective Baer, I think he said. He was in a hurry and didn't ask many questions. Said they were just covering the bases because they already have a suspect. He couldn't tell me who it was, but he said it had nothing to do with the dance school."

"That's good to hear." Hallie smiled. "Could we keep this to ourselves for the moment?"

"You've got it."

"Much appreciated." Sam rose and extended his hand. "If you'll excuse us – tonight's Zumba night."

— Chapter 62 —

HALLIE AND SAM arrived at the ballroom just as Jeff Donegan was demonstrating the newly popular dance-fitness program. He appeared to be creating his own steps: stretching, swaying, adding twists and thrusts to familiar exercises, all moving to a fast Latin beat.

About thirty students from different classes were practicing, trying – without much success – to mimic the rhythmic motions of their teacher.

"Think I'll just watch for a while," Sam whispered, taking a seat at the back of the hall. Hallie nodded, excused herself, and joined the students. It was strictly do-it-yourself dancing, she decided, and fell into her own free style. When the music ended, Jeff clapped his hands for attention. "You were all wonderful," he said breathlessly. "Let's take a break."

No sooner had Hallie dropped into a chair alongside Sam, than a voice called her name. Looking up, she saw a young woman smiling at her. The stranger was extremely pretty, with dark hair pulled back in a ponytail. A tight T-shirt and jeans revealed a slim but curvy figure.

"You don't recognize me," said the woman. "I'm Polly Jane Hodges from Wichita, Kansas. And before that, Polina Belnikov from Moscow."

"Oh, my God!" Sam jumped up to embrace her. "You're gorgeous! You look fantastic!"

Hallie was next to give her a hug. "Polly, what a lovely surprise!"

She grinned. "I came tonight just to see you both. Jeff told me you'd be here. Can we go somewhere after class and get a cup of coffee?"

"We can go now," Hallie whispered. "Sam isn't big on Zumba, and neither am I. Jeff's busy with that blonde. Let's sneak away."

# — Chapter 63 —

THE COFFEE SHOP down the block was almost empty when the three entered and seated themselves at a table.

"Let's see," said Hallie. "Last time I saw you, Polly, you –"

"Polly Jane," she corrected.

"Okay, Polly Jane. It was mid-March – almost three months ago. You said you'd call when you were feeling better, but I never heard from you."

"I wanted to wait till my hair grew back after the chemo, and I hoped to have some good news. Fortunately, I do. The doctor thinks my cancer's gone." Two drops trickled down her cheek. "Mostly…I want to thank you both for saving my life and turning it around. Without you – I'd be dead now."

"Glad we could help." Sam refrained from reminding her how difficult she was. "What happened after you left the hospital?"

She wiped a tear. "Well, as you may remember, I was released from the hospital to a halfway house, but my cancer was still there and I was sent back for surgery. The last time I saw you, Hallie, I was getting chemo and seeing a speech pathologist to help restore my voice."

"You were quite insistent that you wanted to make a new life for yourself. Sam and I prayed you'd do so. And you obviously have."

Polly Jane beamed. "Thanks, I'm very happy. I've a full-time job as spokesperson for the oral cancer group. I go around to schools and speak to the students about the dangers of oral sex and getting infected with HPV, the human papillomavirus. Twenty-one percent of oral cancer patients also show up with lymph nodal metastasis."

"I'm impressed," said Hallie. "You even speak doctor-talk."

"The facts are scary, but there is a vaccine. I've been interviewed on radio, and right now we're working on a documentary. We want to reach as many people as we can. By the way, do you think Tobias would let me speak to the dance classes? I'd only take ten minutes in each class."

"You'll have to ask him," said Sam. "You must have a gift for public speaking."

"No." She blushed. "What I have is an incredible voice teacher who's been coaching me. He corrects my grammar and mispronounced words, tells me where to look at the audience, how to get their attention, and all sorts of 'secrets' to be an effective speaker."

"This voice teacher," said Hallie. "Do I sense something more?"

Polly Jane showed her left hand. A ring with a small round diamond shone brightly. "He's the most fantastic man I've ever known! We're getting married at City Hall later this month. I always wanted to be a June bride."

"Congratulations!" said Sam. "Where will you live?"

"Right now we're living at his house in the Richmond district. I didn't want to get married till all my tattoos were gone, but laser removal takes a year or so, and he didn't want to wait. I'd love to have you meet him."

"Absolutely," said Hallie, "we'll make a date."

Polly Jane turned to Sam with a twinkle. "Speaking

of romance, how's your love life these days? Still a bachelor?"

He laughed. "Thanks to Hallie, I met a charming woman, an opera singer. I'm still single, but that could change. What about you and Jeff? You're friends again?"

"*Just* friends. I apologized for stealing his car and he's forgiven me. He's trying to turn his life around, too. It'd be great if he could buy the dance school."

Sam started to speak but a look from Hallie silenced him. "Tobias mentioned that possibility," she said casually. "I hope Jeff can find the money."

"He says he can. He's determined to do this. Umm – please don't say anything. I forgot I'm not supposed to tell anyone."

"Mum's the word."

They chatted for another half hour, exchanged email addresses, and agreed to meet again.

## — Chapter 64 —

Early the next morning, Hallie left a phone message for TB, saying she had new information. Experience had taught her to add a tease or he wouldn't call back.

He took the bait and phoned her direct line at the office. "What's your information?"

"Oh, hi, TB." He had even less patience than she did. "It's about the Carlie Gaines' case. You apparently visited her dance school. I take a class there. I learned last night that Carlie was thinking about buying the school."

"So?"

"So it seems that some of the dance teachers also want

126

to buy the school, and are trying to raise the money. What if they'd heard Carlie was a competitor and was rich enough to pay the asking price?"

"Do you know this as a fact or are you guessing?"

His skepticism no longer unnerved her. "Last night a friend and I had coffee with an ex-girlfriend of our instructor, Jeff Donegan. She told us – in confidence – that Jeff really wants to buy the school."

"And you're thinking that gave him a motive to kill Carlie. Isn't that a bit far-fetched?"

"Not at all. Strange things were happening at the school: a fancy paperweight disappeared from the owner's desk, objects went missing from lockers, toilets were stopped up, someone even poured so much dance wax on the floor that a woman slipped and broke her leg. I'm guessing these things were done purposely to lower the value of the property. They stopped right after Carlie was killed. If we could get a warrant to search Jeff's house, we might find some of the missing goods."

"A warrant? Are you crazy? What Judge is going to give me that? Where's your evidence?"

"My gut."

"With all due respect, Hallie…"

"I know. My gut isn't evidence. And I know you're convinced that Herb Gaines is your killer, but being the excellent detective that you are, I'm sure you wouldn't want to overlook other possibilities. Would you at least consider talking to Jeff Donegan?"

He sighed. "Yeah, sure. Give me a week or so."

## Chapter 65

HALLIE WASN'T ABOUT to wait a week or so. If she could dream up an excuse, she'd talk to Jeff herself. That Tuesday, she drove her own car to dance class, sensing that he'd be friendlier if Sam weren't there.

Assuring Jeff that it was nothing personal, she asked if they could meet after class. Since he was on the alert for investors, he readily accepted, and shortly after six that evening, sat down with her in the empty ballroom.

"Sure I can't buy you a hot coffee down the street?" he asked, smiling.

Good, she thought. He was turning on the charm. "No, thanks, Jeff, I want to chat with you alone. I'll get right to the point. There's a rumor that you're thinking of buying the school."

He laughed. "Boy, if you want to get a message out, just tell people it's a secret. I guess there's talk going around, huh? I have been keeping my eye open for investors. In fact, I was hoping that's why you want to talk. Might you be interested?"

"No, sorry. I have zero interest. My main preoccupation these days is helping the police find out who murdered Carlie."

"Murdered?" His face froze. "Hell, don't look at me!"

"It's not my call."

"Jeez, Hallie, do the police think I killed Carlie because she wanted to buy the school?"

Surprised that he picked up on it so fast, she decided to use his fears to advantage. "To be honest, the detective told me all the instructors are suspects. The police are looking into your backgrounds. Apparently Tobias reported strange goings-on at the school before Carlie died."

"Whew!" Jeff drew out a white handkerchief and wiped his forehead. "That was a false alarm – just coincidences. Since then, Tobias found his 'missing' paperweight, and dumb-ass Fernando's watch turned up in his locker under a sweater. Tobias put up signs in the restrooms not to toss paper towels in the toilet and we haven't had any plumbing problems since then."

"What about the graffiti? The dance wax?"

"Tobias hired a couple of kids to erase the graffiti and it hasn't come back. The dance wax, I'm afraid, was my fault. I didn't know the janitor had waxed the floor earlier; I forgot that I'd added more, and it was just too much. All these things seemed to happen at the same time, so we jumped to the wrong conclusion. No one was trying to sabotage the school."

What convenient explanations, she thought. "Still – isn't it possible, Jeff, that someone *was* trying to discourage Carlie from becoming the new owner? What about Fernando – is he interested in buying?"

"God forbid! That guy's a real piece of work. Just yelled at me about the Zumba class. Says I'm intruding on his territory. Like he owns every bleeping Latin dance?"

"Maybe he wants to own the whole school."

Jeff shrugged. "I guess anything's possible if Rhoda – his girlfriend, and I use the term loosely – wants to bankroll him. I still think it was a series of coincidences. By the way, that cockroach Fernando was always hitting on Carlie. She was nice to him because Carlie was nice to everyone."

"Did she ever go out with him?"

"I hope not! She once told me he had B.O. – ya know, body odor? – but she was still flirty-flirty with him, always left the door open."

"Why do you think she did that?"

"I know why. If she really wanted to buy the school, she wouldn't have wanted to lose him as a teacher. He seems to ooze some sort of slimy sex appeal. Fernando has the brains of a rodent but the bastard can dance. He's won more tango contests than he can count. And if you want a murder suspect, he gets my vote – rejected lover and all that crap."

He paused to exhale. "Jeez, Hallie, will you tell that big police guy that I had nothing to do with what happened to Carlie?"

"You can tell him yourself, Jeff. His name's TB, and he'll be here next week."

*PART 8*

# — Chapter 66 —

NATE GARCHIK, Hallie learned the next day, remembered that Carlie had once asked him about buying the dance school. She was particularly impressed with their nonprofit foundation for school children.

He'd discouraged her for many reasons, she'd said she'd think it over, and hadn't mentioned it again. But he was quick to agree that if Carlie's interest in becoming the new owner had been known, a competitor might want her out of the running.

A week later, on Wednesday, the 15th of June, Cas invited Margot and Sam to dinner to celebrate Hallie's 35th birthday. The four enjoyed fresh-cooked petrale in a corner table at the Big Four on California Street. Seeing Sam's happy face, Hallie lifted an eyebrow ever so slightly. Margot caught the gesture and answered with an equally subtle nod, which neither man noticed.

Good, thought Hallie. They've slept together.

Dinner talk centered on politics, books, and Sam's announcement that he'd arranged for Polly Jane Hodges to speak to the various dance classes on Friday. Then Margot asked, "Any news about the murder?"

"Not really." Hallie shrugged. "Sam, Detective TB, and Carlie's fiancé Nate Garchik, all think her father, Herb Gaines, or her dance teacher and would-be lover, Jeff Donegan, had motives. Gaines could profit financially, and Jeff wouldn't have any competition buying the dance studio. I can't think of anyone else who'd want her dead."

"I can," said Margot. "Didn't you say she was getting married as soon as she got rid of her other boyfriends? 'Hell hath no fury like a gentleman scorned.' Why not find out who else she rejected?"

"Well, I know Fernando Ruiz, the salsa teacher, was one. Jeff told me she kept him dangling. Most of the others in her black book she only saw once or twice, and according to Nate, she didn't lead them on."

"She was a lovely, refreshingly honest woman," said Sam. "Men were drawn to her. My vote is for Herb Gaines. Jeff Donegan talks a lot, but I doubt he's clever enough to plan a murder that leaves so few clues."

Cas tapped his glass. "Screw the bleeping murder! Tonight we're celebrating my beautiful wife and her coming of age, so to speak. May I offer a toast to the sweetest, smartest, sexiest, snoopiest woman I've ever had the good fortune to marry? May all your dreams and wishes come true, my darling, and may you solve your mystery soon, so we can live happily ever after for a change. I love you."

They kissed, all raised their glasses, and for the moment, Carlie Gaines' unfortunate demise was forgotten.

— Chapter 67 —

As scheduled, Polly Jane Hodges showed up at the Dance School that Friday evening, spoke to Hallie and Sam's class for five minutes, answered questions for another five, then snapped a group picture, and went on to the next class. The students were receptive, and pleased with her offer to send jpegs to all who supplied their email addresses.

Two photos reached Hallie a week later – one of her dance class, and the other was the salsa class, with a note on the back.

"I showed this picture to my fiancé," Polly Jane had written, "and he recognized a former patient. The man had come to him for help getting rid of his Spanish accent. He said the guy was a big ego and full of anger.

"I was interested because he was an instructor, and I heard him grumble that when he owned the dance school, he wouldn't allow strangers (like me) to speak to the students. I don't know if that's helpful, but I circled his picture. XX Polly J."

The ring around Fernando Ruiz's head gave Hallie pause. Intrigued as she was, she saw no reason to bother Sam or TB with this new and possibly useless information.

She believed Jeff's statement that Carlie had rejected Fernando, and she had no doubt that Polly Jane had over-heard Fernando talk about buying the dance school – a re-mark he could well have made in jest.

Yet here was another possible suspect with not one, but two motives – Carlie's rejection, and a desire to own the school! And still, she was stumped. After scrutinizing both pictures, and spotting nothing unusual, she found Cas at his computer.

"Darling," she said, "Would you mind glancing at these pictures and tell me what you see?"

He spun around in his chair and took the photos. "What are you looking for?"

"I don't know. I'm baffled. I hoped these images might give me some insight into the people in the dance classes. Any one of them could be involved in Carlie's death."

"Who's the man circled?"

"That's Fernando Ruiz, the salsa teacher. Does he look violent to you?"

"You mean would I fear blunt force trauma from his piñata? Probably not."

"Be serious, Cas! I really need your help. I've gone through all my clues a dozen times, and I keep coming back to the dance school. I'm convinced the answer to Carlie's murder is there."

"Your gut again?" He patted her tummy. "It's a busy little gut but a cute one."

"Darn you," she growled, settling down on his knee. "You're hopeless."

"Probably. But I have an idea. Remember that psychic woman you saw last year?"

"Zlotta Kofiszny? 'The world's leading celebrity psychic'? Why bring her up? You're a worse skeptic than I am."

He nodded agreement. "They're all fakes – especially the ones who claim to see the future. But I watched Zlotta on TV a few weeks ago, and she's a damn good fake – amazingly observant and intuitive. She reads people well. Why not take your pictures to her? It can't hurt."

"Only my wallet," she laughed. "I never thought I'd hear you recommend a psychic, but…it's not a bad idea."

She hugged him and jumped off his knee. "Thanks, sweetheart. I'll go make an appointment. I'm suddenly feeling very spiritual."

*PART 9*

## — Chapter 68 —

Saturday, June 25th was a memorable day in New York. Gov. Andrew M. Cuomo had signed a same-sex marriage bill into law the night before, marking the end of a heated campaign.

That morning, Hallie called Sam with the good news. His surprised stammering told her he was probably in bed, and not alone.

"I knew you'd be pleased for your daughter's sake," she said, pretending not to notice his discomfort. "I've got to run now, but we'll talk later. Oh, and give my love to Margot."

## — Chapter 69 —

ZLOTTA KOFISZNY, the self-proclaimed "World's Leading Celebrity Psychic," lived and worked in a gray stucco Victorian on Bush Street, midway between Hallie's home and downtown San Francisco.

Hallie had spent most of the July 4th weekend helping the nanny take care of her twin nieces, Coco and Mandy. Fortunately, their parents were back from their trip, and the next day, Hallie kept her long-awaited appointment with Zlotta Kofiszny.

The house was much as she remembered it, plain and nondescript, save for a dove of peace under the address plate. The bell was answered almost immediately.

"Welcome back, sister Hallie," smiled a short, stout man, garbed in head-to-toe black. "I'm Rev. Barney of the Church of Serenity. We've been expecting you."

"Thanks, I do have an appointment."

"Forgive me. What I meant is that Madame Zlotta knew you were coming back to us. She told me so at the beginning of the year – said it would be either July or September."

"She was right, as usual. Nice to see you again, Reverend." Her eyes rested momentarily on his hairless head; he'd reminded her of a round smiley face the first time they met – and still did.

"Thank you, sister Hallie." He led the way towards a table covered with brochures. "Madame Zlotta will be with you shortly. Your donation to the church will be a hundred dollars for a thirty minute reading, only fifty for the second half hour."

She resisted saying, "I'll take the second half hour."

He went on: "Should you wish the candle ceremony to protect you from negative spirits, it's only eighty dollars."

"Just the reading, please." What a rip-off! She hoped Cas wouldn't ask what she paid.

After returning her credit card, Rev. Barney pushed aside a purple curtain leading to a windowless room. A single candle on a round table provided the only lighting. The scent of incense was strong. Ravel's *Bolero* played softly in the background.

As before, Hallie took one of two chairs and glanced around. Nothing had changed. Painted walls echoed the magentas of the faded Persian carpet. A portrait of a much younger "Madame Zlotta" dominated the room, her eyes seemingly fixed on the observer. Photos and clippings from various publications competed for space on another wall.

The sound of footsteps alerted Hallie – and then, a surprise. The fashionable tweed pantsuit Zlotta had worn previously had been replaced by a flowery blouse tucked into a floor-length red skirt. Her short white hair had grown long enough to be pulled back in a bun. Gold loop earrings framed a wrinkled, once-pretty face.

She smiled and offered a hand. "Welcome, my dear. I see you're troubled. Would you like some tea?"

"No, thanks." The time clock was ticking in her brain. No way would she pay for overtime. "May I tell you why I came to see you?"

They both sat down. "Please do. I'm here to help."

— Chapter 70 —

As BRIEFLY as she could, Hallie recounted the facts, starting with discovering Carlie's body, and up to the present. The psychic often interrupted with questions, stretching out the time.

Finally, Hallie reached into a briefcase and brought out the two pictures. "I know you read people," she said. "I wonder if you'd look at these photos from the dance school and tell me if anyone or anything strikes you as unusual."

Nodding, Zlotta took a magnifying glass from a needlepoint case and set the pictures on the table before her. She stared a long moment at the first one, then at the second, then back to the first. Five minutes passed.

Finally, she looked up. "My dear," she said softly, "what you ask is not simple. These are complicated people, each with his or her own set of pasts and futures. I do see some trouble spots – this man, for instance, is some sort of leader of the group. He's prone to exaggeration and lies."

She was pointing to Jeff. "And this sad young woman has a husband or lover who abuses her. The man next to her worries about his teeth. However, I cannot possibly study all these people and give you quick answers. Can you leave the pictures with me? I won't charge you for the extra time. I know you are trying to find closure for the lawyer who loved this poor woman."

"That's most kind of you, Madame Zlotta."

"Now, my child, give me your hand."

Hallie obliged.

The psychic's voice dropped suddenly, as if she were speaking from a distance. "The forces of good have conquered the shadows of darkness and brought you back to me. They know that you are troubled. Your vibrations tell me another person is involved. Your husband?"

"No." Gently withdrawing her hand, Hallie glanced at her watch. Five minutes to go. "My personal life is quite happy. I came to see you about this case. When might you have some thoughts to share?"

"I'll have to call you, my dear. I'll need time to consult a helper. She will clarify what's weighing you down."

"Nothing –" She stopped herself.

"I know you *think* you came here to talk about your friend. The evil spirits have clouded your mind and must be cast away. But not today. I sense you're anxious to leave. If you're as smart as I know you are –"

Hallie smiled and stood up. "Afraid I do have to go. Thanks, Madame Zlotta. I'll wait to hear from you."

# — Chapter 71 —

THE NEXT MORNING, back in her office, Hallie took two calls. One was from Margot, telling her that Sam's daughter Athena was getting married in New York on July 25th, the first day the gay marriage law would take effect. Sam would be flying there for the wedding, and had invited Margot to go along. Hallie was pleased that her matchmaking efforts – so far – had succeeded.

No sooner had she hung up when Ken, her assistant, buzzed. "You'll want this call," he said.

He was right. TB's loud voice boomed in her ear. "Finally got a break in the case," he reported. "We picked up Herb Gaines last night."

"Where? How?"

"The same place where he met Freddy Fedora. The bartender had been keeping an eye out for him. He texted me when Gaines walked in. I'm sure he's our man."

"Have you questioned him?"

"No, he lawyered up. We're waiting for her now."

"May I come peek through the window?"

"What took you so long to ask?"

"I'll be right there!"

# — Chapter 72 —

**Herb Gaines** was not at all what Hallie expected. Instead of a bent-over, hirsute old man in shabby clothes, the suspect stood almost six feet tall, well-dressed in a dark suit and open-collared shirt. If one could ignore the leathery skin, reddish complexion, and deep scar from upper lip to left eye, he was not unattractive. And despite a few wrinkles and gray hair, he looked younger than his seventy years.

Hallie and Police Lieutenant Helen Kaiser peered anxiously through the one-way glass. Herb Gaines, rubbing his handcuff-bruised wrists, and his lawyer, Sloane – a tight-lipped brunette – came into the room and sat down opposite TB. His partner, Lenny, stood by the door.

"Why have you been avoiding us?" was TB's first question.

Gaines smiled. "I was busy."

"Doing what?"

"This and that."

TB struggled for patience. "What do you live on, Mr. Gaines?"

"I had some money saved when I came here from France a few months ago. And then my daughter – my poor, sweet Carlie – gave me some money."

"Twenty-five thousand, I hear."

"That's correct, Officer. She wanted to help me get back on my feet."

"And that's the only reason she gave you the money?"

"That's the only reason. Whatever Freddy Fedora told you is a lie."

"He said you hired him to steal her iPad. He said it showed that Carlie paid you that money to keep out of her life. He said she asked her lawyer to write you out of her will."

"Nonsense," Gaines said firmly. "First of all, sure, Carlie and I had issues – what family doesn't? And secondly,

Carlie's lawyer admits she had no will, so how could she write me out of something that doesn't exist?"

"The so-called 'evidence' Mr. Fedora claims he stole is worthless," interjected attorney Sloane. "Everything he says is hearsay."

TB ignored her and looked to Gaines. "You and Freddy Fedora had a fight in a bar. What was that about?"

"We had a sports bet. My team lost, I gave him a hundred bucks. He said we bet a thousand. He's a liar."

"And you had nothing to do with his stealing your daughter's iPad?"

"Why would I offer that drunken bum a grand? And I don't have any iPad he claims he gave me. Freddy read about Carlie's death in the paper, knew she was my daughter and thought he could make some quick bucks. He told me he pretended to be her brother to get the iPad, and that the machine had 'incriminating evidence.' He wanted five grand for the damn thing. I told him to go you-know-what."

TB sighed loudly. He was getting nowhere. "You told him to get lost because you learned that the police knew about the theft. That meant the information on the iPad was stolen evidence that couldn't be used in a court of law. Now you're claiming that you're the rightful heir and entitled to your daughter's estate. And she's not around to say otherwise. Isn't that why you murdered her, Mr. Gaines?"

"Hold on!" cried an angry Sloane. "My client has a foolproof alibi. He was out of town the week before and after Carlie died."

"So what? He could afford to hire someone. Or maybe he gave her a slow-acting poison before he left."

"That's enough." She grabbed Gaines' arm and pulled him to his feet. "You have no reason to keep my client here. He's still grieving over his loss and you are insulting him and accusing him without the slightest bit of evidence. We'll pay the fines for disturbing the peace." She threw her card on the table. "You know how to reach me."

"Don't leave town, Mr. Gaines," ordered TB. "We aren't through with you."

— Chapter 73 —

AFTER DANCE CLASS, two Tuesdays later, Hallie gave Sam a hug, wished him and Margot a happy trip to New York, and hurried down the hall to a larger ballroom, where Fernando Ruiz was teaching. The week before, she'd asked if she could visit one of his classes, and he'd responded enthusiastically.

At the time, she wondered if Fernando thought she might be coming on to him, if he liked the idea of stealing one of Jeff's pupils, or if he was simply turning on the charm for a prospective student. Maybe all three.

The large size of the class surprised her. Counting quickly, she saw eighteen women dancing solo and seven male-female couples on the floor, moving to the fast Brazilian beat. Fernando led the group with a Hispanic woman, hips and pelvises swaying non-stop.

Spotting Hallie in the doorway, he shouted, "Samba, SamBAH!" and motioned her inside.

She waved and headed for a bench, but the music was seductive, and she couldn't resist joining the dancers. Her eyes focused on Fernando as she tried to imitate him, marveling at his grace and flexibility. He was a far smoother and sexier dancer than Jeff. No wonder Jeff was jealous.

Rhoda Starr-Stevens, who had dropped out of Jeff's classes at Fernando's request, was in the crowd, a few feet away. She noted Hallie's interchange with Fernando, and gave her a nod of recognition.

Hallie smiled back, wondering if Rhoda ever felt out of place among all the young people in their sweats. On the contrary, she seemed quite at ease, with her dyed blonde hair and sparkling jewelry, squeezed into designer duds, twisting, turning, wiggling her hips with – alas – the grace of an elephant.

As the class ended, Hallie saw Rhoda blow a kiss to Fernando, then leave. When she was safely out of sight, he approached his visitor.

"*Señora* Marsh," he gushed, "How pleasing! I see you dance – you are very good. You should learn tango. You would be *magnifica!*"

Hallie smiled. "Thanks. If you're not too busy, I'd love a few words with you. Could I buy you a cup of coffee?"

"*Si, si, con mucho gusto.*"

"Rhoda won't mind?"

"No, no, she has date with old husband…how you say?"

"We say 'ex-husband.' "

"Ah, *graçias*. So I have whole night. Where we go?"

"Just down the street."

Fearful he would take her arm, she led the way, walking fast. He seemed to get the hint, and followed her into the café and a corner table.

They gave their orders, then Hallie wasted no time. "Fernando," she said, "you heard about Carlie Gaines?"

"*Si, si*," he answered with a long face. "A great sadness. She was so beautiful."

"You knew her well?"

"No, no, only friends. Why you ask?"

"Carlie did not die a natural death. She was murdered. Someone killed her."

"I hear that. *Dios mio*! Who would keel such pretty lady?"

"That's what I'm trying to help the police find out."

His face brightened. "Ah, *la policia*. I talk to your detective. He ask too many questions."

"Did he ask if you wanted to buy the school?"

"Yes. He ask if my sweetheart Rhoda was – how you say – lend money to buy school. I say I hope yes. Since I was small boy, I want to own dance school. You like tango?"

"I don't know how –"

"I teach you. Tomorrow we have *milonga* – tango party. You meet *muchos tangueros*. You come?"

"Sorry, no thanks. Who else wants to buy the school?"

He shrugged. "I think Jeff, maybe also teachers."

"Do you want it badly?"

"I want it, yes." His eyes widened. "If Jeff buy school, I geev notice. I no work for him. But *Señora*, if Carlie had buy school, that okay. Maybe Jeff keel her."

Hallie perked up. "Do you have any reason to think that Jeff might have harmed her?"

"He is bad man."

Fernando would say no more on the subject. His efforts to get personal failed, and Hallie thanked him for his time, explaining that her husband was awaiting her at home. Fernando insisted on walking her to her car, parked on the street. He watched her climb inside, blew a kiss and strolled off.

As Hallie started the engine, she noticed a shiny black Mercedes parked a block away. The scarf and dark glasses did little to hide the identity of the woman in the passenger's seat. Pretending not to see or recognize her, Hallie pressed the accelerator and drove home.

— Chapter 74 —

THE NEXT DAY, Wednesday, brought the call Hallie had been waiting for. Two weeks since Zlotta Kofiszny had agreed to look at the dance class pictures, and show them to "a helper," the psychic finally had some "revelations."

Frustrated at having seen the pile of active cases on detective TB's desk, and realizing that solving Carlie's murder was not a top priority for the police, Hallie had no qualms about continuing her own investigation.

Zlotta agreed to see her that Friday, and at ten a.m. promptly, she rang the bell of the now-familiar Victorian. After greeting "Reverend Barney of the Church of Serenity," she paid another hundred dollar fee, plus an extra seventy-five for "Madame's channeller." With a resigned-but-hopeful sigh, Halie sank into a chair in the salon.

The psychic was quick to arrive, this time garbed in full gypsy regalia, from her red turban and hoop earrings down to her Birkenstocks. "Hope I didn't keep you waiting, my dear," she said, sitting down. "The TV folks are coming at eleven-thirty to do an interview, and I wanted to be sure you and I had enough time together. I'm not fond of dressing up in this silly costume, but it's what they wanted."

"You look very colorful," said Hallie, aware that the timer on the table was already clicking.

Zlotta noticed her glance and switched it off. "No worries about the clock today," she said, smiling. "I was inspired by my beloved Dysma."

"Dizma?" The name sounded like a disease.

"D-Y-S-M-A. My connection to the spiritual world. Her divine presence was a great help with your pictures. Shall we get right to them?"

"I can't wait." So Dysma was "Madame's channeller." Dare she ask why a divine presence needed seventy-five bucks? And what happened to her offer not to charge extra?

Zlotta mumbled a few words that sounded like, *"Vox deeldo hacienda,"* then pressed a button. A bright beam shone down on the two pictures laid out on the table.

"Come sit beside me, dear child. Together, we will solve your murder."

— Chapter 75 —

THE ROOM was silent several minutes, save for the psychic's heavy breathing. Then she took Hallie's hand, mumbled something incoherent, and spoke in a soft tone.

"Your killer is a man," she began, enunciating each word. "This man was intimate with the victim. No one knew

148

their secret. This man loved her."

"Did she love him?"

"That is doubtful. I was not given the identity of this man. I do not know if he is in these pictures. But I will tell you what I see. Do you know the expression 'cold reading?'"

"Like – for an audition?"

"Yes. It's also a psychic term, sometimes used negatively, to describe a technique. It means that we analyze body language, age, hair style, facial expression, clothing, race, gender, and more, when we're giving a reading. We make assumptions based on our intuition and experience. And we listen to what the spirits tell us."

"Are they usually right?"

"Oh, yes. You see, my dear, one can only become clairvoyant by turning off one's thinking and turning on one's senses. I'm a psychic medium. I connect with beings on both sides. When I give a reading, I make a few observations, then my mind goes blank. I wait for other thoughts to come in."

"And do they?"

"Indeed they do. The spirits are free souls, sometimes playful, sometimes testing us, sometimes deliberately leading us astray. Dysma does her best to control them, but it's not always possible."

The psychic paused. "I sense your impatience, Hallie. I want you to know that the spirits sometimes resent having paper images instead of actual persons to read. But let's move on."

"Please do." Hallie pointed to the picture of her class. "What do you see?"

"I see much. I see this man who is leading the class. His clothes are revealing. He and the victim were intimate. His name?"

"Jeff Donegan. He's the instructor and a big ego."

"He may have harmed Carlie."

"Is he the killer?" asked Hallie.

"He could be. He is in conflict with this man." Zlotta moved to the second picture. "He, too, seems to be the leader of the class."

"That's Fernando Ruiz, the salsa teacher."

"They are not friends. Fernando is also a narcissist, but weaker, kinder, more generous. And I see other men not in these pictures. Carlie was active sexually, though she only gave her body, never her soul."

"Not even to her fiancé?"

"Not to anyone. He may also be a suspect. She frustrated her lovers. One of them killed her."

Zlotta returned to the first picture, of Jeff's class, and focused on the students, suggesting their various interests, emotional states, and in one case, that the woman was a Lesbian. Then she moved to the second picture, of Fernando's class, and stared a long minute before speaking. "Who is this person in the front row?"

"That's Rhoda Starr-Stevens – a friend of Fernando's."

"And a good deal more, my dear. He did not buy that gold watch on a dance teacher's salary."

"Very astute."

"Miss or Mrs. Rhoda, overweight, over-age, over-dressed and overloaded with jewelry stands out among the younger people in their workout clothes. Why would she be there if not to keep an eye on her lover? And those beads she's wearing…"

"Yes?"

"They look familiar, red with a black dot. We must find out more, but I'm not getting any answers."

Zlotta clasped her hands and looked up pleadingly. "Dysma, dear friend, tell the spirits I don't understand what they're telling me. What? Yes, I know my mind is cluttered. Give me a minute."

Hallie sat quietly as the psychic bowed her head and appeared to concentrate. After what seemed forever to Hallie, she opened her eyes and spoke in a sad voice: "They've gone."

"The spirits?"

"They don't like to linger in one place. And they were unhappy that I wasn't connecting with any beings in their world. So they decided to contact a man named R. Stuart Marsh. I believe he was – your father."

## — Chapter 76 —

As ZLOTTA'S WORDS sank in, Hallie froze. The woman was behaving strangely, sometimes speaking frankly, other times reverting to her otherworldly nonsense.

But now she had gone too far. Hallie had made peace with her father's death thirteen years ago; she didn't need reminders of her loss.

"Forgive my honesty, Madame Zlotta, but I'm not interested. I told you the first time I saw you that I'm a skeptic and I haven't changed. I don't believe that dead people talk to you any more than I believe that you read minds. But as you admitted, you're excellent at reading faces and body language, and you've given me a lot to think about."

"Shhh." Zlotta put her fingers to her lips. "Release your fears, my dear. No one will intrude on your memories of your father. And whether you believe it or not, you've just had a visitation. I saw R. Stuart Marsh for a flash of a second – a handsome man with a head of gray hair. I saw you reach up and touch your forehead as if you were brushing something away. That was your father, letting you know he's always with you. When you swept him off your face, he knew you felt his kiss. And he was a happy man."

Hallie relaxed. It was all too absurd to take seriously. "I guess he was a lot younger if he had a full head of hair," she joked. "Thanks for your time, Madame Zlotta. Good luck in your TV interview. I'm off, now, to ponder your revelations."

"Come back soon, my dear. I believe this is yours." The psychic handed her a small envelope.

With a grateful wave, Hallie took the offering, grabbed her pictures and disappeared through the beaded curtains.

— Chapter 77 —

HURRYING DOWN the street, Hallie's curiosity got the better of her decision to wait till she was in the car. Tearing open the envelope, she pulled out a white receipt – a credit on her Visa card for seventy-five dollars!

She stared in disbelief. It was impossible! She hadn't

left Zlotta's salon during the hour, and Rev. Barney hadn't been in there. Could she have read Hallie's mind? Could she have seen her unhappiness at being charged seventy-five dollars when she said there would be no charge? Whatever the reason, whatever trick Zlotta used to pull it off, Hallie was pleased that Zlotta had kept her word.

Once in the car, Hallie looked more closely at the receipt and saw that the date was correct, but the time was off by a little over an hour.

Then it became clear: it had all been planned in advance! Rev. Barney would charge her extra, then a few minutes later, credit her with the same amount, and somehow slip the receipt to Zlotta. A more gullible person might believe that Zlotta had actually read her mind.

Back home at her desk, Hallie realized that Sam Butler was in New York with Margot, Detective TB was "up to my eyeballs in homicides," Cas was on a plane to Washington, and Nate Garchik, if she could trust anything Zlotta said, should be treated as a suspect. But what motive could he possibly have?

True, Nate was the court-appointed "Administrator of the Decedent's Estate," and in charge of distributing Carlie's assets. He was also getting $500 an hour for his efforts – he hardly needed Carlie's money. Besides, his anguish had seemed so real...he couldn't have faked that. Could he possibly have been grieving for the terrible thing he'd done?

Her brain was whirling as she set the pictures on a table and sat down at her computer, determined to record the psychic's "revelations" while they were fresh. The cell phone startled her.

"Hi, honey," she heard Cas say. "We just landed at Dulles, and I'm waiting for a cab to downtown D.C. How was your séance?"

"Oh, darling, I'm glad you're safe." Hallie reached for her notes. "Zlotta was nutty as always. I'm about to type my scribbles. Wait, here's a good one. She looked at the picture of our class and said that Sandralee James is gay – as if you could tell from a person's face."

"Where have you been, my fearless snooper? Better Google 'gaydar' – that stands for 'gay radar' – and enlighten yourself. We ran a story from Reuters last week, stating that some people are quite accurate at spotting sex preferences just from faces."

"Really? You can look at someone and tell –"

"Gotta run, honey. My cab's here. Love you. Call later." And he was gone.

*PART 10*

# — Chapter 78 —

HALLIE sat staring at her computer screen. Having recorded the psychic's various musings, suggestions and conclusions, she pulled a paper from the printer and looked it over. Zlotta had insisted that Carlie's killer was male, had loved her, bedded her and murdered her – maybe in that order.

What next? A glance at the clock told her it was time to dress. The San Francisco Dance Studio was closing for a week before starting its summer season, and owner Tobias Miller was hosting his annual "Two-Step Ball" for teachers, students, and their significant others.

Slipping into her favorite pink Chanel suit – "Your uniform" Cas called it – she fussed with her hair, make-up, the contents of her purse, and finally decided she felt confident enough to attend the party alone. Having neither Cas nor Sam to escort her, she decided she would make a quick appearance and depart.

Her first surprise was seeing a pair of faux marble columns wrapped in roses outside the school entrance. Floral genius Stanlee Gatti's handiwork was hard to miss.

The ballroom was a stunning forest of red "bushes" and overhanging garlands. Towering over the well-dressed crowd, tall, blond Lucas Schoemaker, caterer Dan McCall's executive chef, waved her a greeting.

Impressive, she thought. Tobias is sparing no expense. A server materialized, offered her sparkling water, wine or champagne. She chose Perrier.

"No bubbly tonight, Hallie?" Jeff Donegan peered over the waiter's shoulder and grinned a welcome. "Where's your school spirit?"

"I'm my designated driver," she smiled, immediately regretting her words.

"What, no Sam? No husband? Who's going to watch after you?"

"I'll manage. By the way, you look almost respectable in your suit and tie."

Her teasing escaped him. He loosened his collar. "Thanks, but this damn shirt is killing me. Care to dance?"

"Well, I just —"

He took her glass and set it on a table. "Now you have no excuse."

"I guess not."

The floor was crowded with couples swaying to "All the Things You Are." Hallie recognized Gary Zellerbach's band on the stage.

"Old Tobias is going all out tonight," Jeff whispered. "Bet he's going to make an announcement. He's been humping the same broad for years."

Hallie pulled slightly back. He was drunker than she'd realized.

"Listen, after the party —" A tap on the shoulder stopped him. He spun around angrily, then changed his expression when he saw who it was. "Hey there, Tobias, old pal. This is one cool bash."

"Thanks, Jeff. Hope you don't mind my cutting in."

The instructor made a sweeping bow. "Be my guest. After all I'm *your* guest, right?" Laughing at his cleverness, he moved away.

Hallie smiled as her new partner circled her waist.

"Thanks, Tobias, you saved me. I made the mistake of telling him Sam and my husband weren't here."

Tobias's eyes twinkled. "I hear he's quite the ladies' man – or would like to be. Thank *you* for coming tonight. I've been meaning to ask if there's any news about Carlie."

Hallie shook her head. "Wish I could say yes, but we're at a standstill. Any thoughts?"

"Just between us, I've wondered about Fernando. I saw him chatting with Carlie in the hall one day. He seemed quite smitten. And she seemed anxious to get away. Latin men don't like to be rejected."

"No..." Two women passed by, greeted Hallie, thanked Tobias, then danced off, cheek-to-cheek. "That brunette – I can't think of her name."

Tobias laughed. "That's Sandralee James. She looks different with makeup and a fancy hairdo. And that's her wife she's dancing with."

"Oh, yes – of course." So Zlotta's 'gaydar' was right. She *could* tell sex preference from just seeing Sandralee's picture. It gave Hallie pause. Could Zlotta also be right saying that Carlie's killer was a man who loved her?

"Will you excuse me, Hallie?" Tobias stopped mid-floor and kissed her cheek. "I have to say a few words."

"I can't wait to hear them."

She watched as he made his way across the room to the bandleader, who handed him a microphone, then signaled for a drum roll.

# — Chapter 79 —

THE ROOM was instantly still. Tobias cleared his throat and began, "My dear friends, I want to welcome you all to what will be my last party at the school."

A moan went through the crowd as the host quickly continued, "This is a happy night for me, and I hope for you, too. Today, I signed the papers, and starting in about two weeks, on Monday, August 8th, the San Francisco Dance Studio will be run by its new owners, the popular Piedmont Ballroom."

Applause broke out. A voice shouted, "Way to go, Tobie!" The speaker raised his hands for silence.

"As many of you know, this has been a tough decision. To those who wonder why I sold to a competitor and not to some of you here tonight, the answer is simple. They were the high bidders – by far. And since I'm retiring, I'm forced to consider my financial future."

More applause.

"Ecclesiastes said, 'There's a time for everything,' and this is my time to spend my remaining years with the woman I love. We plan to travel, enjoy the opera, eat good food, and who knows? We might even make our relationship legal."

The room exploded in cheers. The band struck up, "I'm Getting Married in the Morning," and a young man grabbed Hallie, twirled her around a few times, and danced off.

She glanced across the ballroom. The crowd was well liquored-up, delighted to have an excuse to celebrate. No one seemed concerned about what changes the new owners might make to their school.

Fortunately, that wasn't her worry, either. Having paid her respects to Tobias, she headed for the exit.

— Chapter 80 —

"*HOLA!, CARA.*" Fernando's unmistakable voice made Hallie stop and turn around. "You go home so soon?"

"Oh, hi, Fernando. Yes, my husband's waiting for me." She wasn't about to repeat her mistake. "I'm sorry you weren't able to buy the school. I know how much you wanted it."

He frowned, clenching a fist in the air. "I so mad I could *keel* someone! Ees not fair! I should own school. Tobias never say he want more money! I weesh –" He took a minute to calm himself. Then he lowered his voice. "All my life I want to own school. *Comprendes,* Hallie? I so mad! Maybe go back to Argentina."

"Tobias didn't mean to hurt you, Fernando."

He started to reply then stopped himself. His lips were still clenched when he handed her his clipboard. "You sign my picture?"

"I wasn't in your class."

"But you are my friend, no?"

"Yes." She took his pen, wrote a few kind words in the margin, and scribbled her name. "You're very photogenic, Fernando. So is Rhoda."

"Ah, my Rhoda."

"That's a lovely necklace she's wearing."

He welcomed a new subject. "You like? I buy that in

South America. Suriname. They grow rosary beads and make pretty jewels."

"You have excellent taste. And you're looking very dapper tonight."

"What is dapper?" He suddenly tensed. "My Rhoda waves, I must go. Good-bye, *cara*."

— Chapter 81 —

A BEEPING answering machine greeted Hallie's return home. The message asked her to phone TB the next morning. Yes, he'd be working on a Saturday.

She called at eight a.m., left a message. He called back shortly after nine.

"It's about the Gaines case," he said. "There's been a new development – another mysterious death. According to the coroner, Dr. Toy, an Italian immigrant named Mario Ingoli appears to have died from the same poison that killed Gaines."

"Oh, dear, how awful! Has Dr. Toy done the autopsy?"

"Yep. The symptoms are the same, the time it took Ingoli to die is about the same, the blood, the tox screen, the diseased organs, even the vomit. Everything mimics Gaines' death. The question is: How do we connect a rich, beautiful young woman with a sixty-two year old garbage collector from Daly City?"

"Maybe he collected her garbage."

"We checked. His route goes from Fillmore to Third Avenue – covers much of Pacific and Presidio Heights, and part of the Inner Richmond. Carlie Gaines lived across town on Russian Hill."

Hallie took a moment to digest the information. Then she asked, "Why are you telling me this, TB? You told me you don't like me to work on your cases."

"I don't. And I told you to stop meddling, but I know you haven't. Carlie's lawyer told me you're helping him find answers so he can close her estate."

"That's right, I am. Nate Garchik doesn't want to settle with Carlie's father until he knows for sure that Daddy didn't do the deed."

"So he told me. We're keeping the file open, but I've got more cases than I can handle and not nearly enough man – er, person power. So if you want to do some *discreet* prying, you have my okay on two conditions: one, you don't put yourself or anyone else in harm's way, and two, you report back to me every day by phone, text or email."

"Deal," she said eagerly. "Did Mr. Ingoli have a wife, and if so, what's her name and address?"

"I'll text you," he said, "Thanks and good-bye."

*PART 11*

## — Chapter 82 —

EARLY Monday morning, Hallie parked her car in front of a white clapboard house on Ocean Drive in Daly City, just South of San Francisco. The property looked clean and well cared-for. A neatly-mowed lawn with a "For Sale" sign led her to the front door.

The woman who opened it was short, plump, and fortyish. Dark hair framed a round, freckled face. "I'm Francesca Ingoli," she said nervously. "You're the lady who's helping the police? My mom's sick and can't see you. C'mon in. 'Scuse the mess. Mom's gonna move in with me."

Hallie stepped around several large boxes to follow her host to a room devoid of furniture, save for two folding chairs. "I'm terribly sorry for your loss."

They sat down facing each other. "It's – like so weird. Dad was never sick. And the dumb doctors don't even know what killed him!" Her eyes welled with tears.

"We're hoping to find that out. What did your Dad do in his free time?"

Francesca shrugged. "Putter. He has – *had* – a half-assed workshop in a shed out back."

"Did he have any other hobbies? A favorite restaurant? Bar? Grocery store? Friends he hung out with?"

"Uh-uh. Dad would be too pooped after work. He'd stuff down some dinner, grab a beer and watch TV. Mom did the shopping and cooking."

"And all he liked to do on weekends was –?"

"Putter. He liked to get stuff – I mean clean stuff like pieces of wood or metal that people threw away. He'd make funny sculptures out of them. I'd show you, but they're all packed away."

"You're saying that sometimes he rescued things from the garbage?"

"Not food or icky stuff. Like – well, a few weeks ago he showed me a hammer he found. It looked brand new. He was using it to make me a book case until he hit his thumb."

"Were you there?"

"I was in the kitchen. I heard him swearing." She giggled. "Mom heard him, too. She got embarrassed – like I never heard those words before?"

"What happened to his thumb?"

"Mom wanted to take him to the hospital, but Dad just wrapped it in a towel and held his hand in the air to stop the bleeding. That was the last day he worked before he got sick."

Hallie was instantly alert. "Do you know where that hammer is now?"

"Those weird men in the white suits must've taken it. They took almost everything from his workshop."

"Was that the hazmat crew from the coroner's office?"

Francesca shrugged. "All I know is that Mom called 911 and said Dad had been awfully sick and throwing up all over, and then, just four days later, he stopped breathing and died. Mom said it looked like his skin was turning blue. The 911 lady said not to touch anything."

"I hope she followed instructions."

"Yeah. Then Mom called me and I came right over. The next thing was these men in white suits came and wrapped everything in plastic bags, including Dad. They wheeled him and his stuff out to a big truck. It was gross!"

"I'm so sorry." Her facts sounded too familiar to be coincidental, especially the blue-tinted skin. Hallie stood up. "Thanks for your time, Francesca, you've been a big help. Please give your Mom my condolences. If I see or hear anything that could help explain your father's death – I'll let you know."

— Chapter 83 —

FOR THE FIRST TIME, Hallie felt she was getting close to finding answers. Back in her office, she rang Dr. Toy to ask him to check with the hazmat team. Could they look for a "brand new" hammer taken from Mr. Ingoli's workshop – possibly one with blood on it? If so, could they check for DNA, prints, and traces of any unusual substances? A long shot, to be sure, but worth checking.

Her second call was to Mr. Ingoli's supervisor. At her request, he faxed over a list of streets and street numbers from Mario Ingoli's last collection route.

Comparing them to the list of addresses she had for students in Jeff's and Fernando's classes, Hallie found three familiar names: Sandralee James, Sam Butler, and Rhoda Starr-Stevens.

None of them was a suspect, yet Rhoda might be able to shed light on Fernando, who was looking more and more suspicious. His anger had seemed extreme. Had he wanted to own the dance school badly enough to kill a rival bidder?

Rhoda was cordial when Hallie called, and invited her for

cocktails. Hallie claimed evening plans and asked if she could come by earlier – presumably when Fernando wouldn't be there. They made a date for three p.m.

— Chapter 84 —

A DOORMAN met Hallie at the entrance to an imposing white building on Pacific Avenue. She couldn't resist asking him – casually, she hoped – if he'd seen her friend Fernando lately.

"Mr. Ruiz lives here," was the polite answer. "I see him and Mrs. Starr-Stevens often."

"Thank you." Hallie had assumed they were living together. It was not an address a dancing instructor could afford. The elevator stopped at the tenth floor, and its passenger stepped into an entranceway filled with orchid plants.

Rhoda was quick to answer her bell. She welcomed Hallie with a double-cheek air kiss, then took her arm. "Here's the library, where Fernando and I spend our time," she said, motioning to a leather sofa. "Make yourself comfortable. What are you drinking?"

"Nothing at the moment, thanks." Hallie was surprised to note that the décor – unlike its owner, squeezed into a black sequined jumpsuit – was tasteful and restrained.

"My late husband was very conservative," Rhoda said, sensing her visitor's curiosity. "He and Fernando were like night and day. Fernando doesn't try to run everything. He lets me be me."

She babbled on for a good ten minutes before Hallie could squeeze in a question: "Did you happen to see your dance class picture?"

167

"Oh, that horrible thing. I look sixty years old."

"I thought you looked attractive." Zlotta's words flashed to mind. "Those lovely beads you were wearing. Is there a story to them?"

"Nothing of interest."

"They seem so unusual. Did you get them here?"

"No. Fernando and I were in South America. We passed a store and the necklace was in the window. I admired it and Fernando bought it for me. I wear it mainly to please him. But I'm talking too much. Tell me, any news about Carlie?"

"Not really," said Hallie. "The police were asking about Jeff Donegan. They had questions about Fernando, too."

"Good Lord! Is he a suspect?"

"Everyone at the school is a suspect. The police have eliminated the men she dated; none had any reason to want her dead. That pretty much leaves her father, and several people who were unhappy that she wanted to buy the school.

"Like Fernando? He's impulsive and unpredictable, and he wanted that school badly, but I don't think he'd kill someone to get it."

"You don't *think*?"

"I mean, I don't understand the Latin temperament. Do you know his background?"

"No."

"Briefly, he grew up in La Pampa, a province of Argentina. His father was a pharmacist, and used to take his son to the store to teach him the business. Unfortunately, Fernando joined a gang, and part of his initiation was to kill a person, which he claims he did. I don't know the details, but he said it haunted him so much, he learned to dance. He mastered the tango and won all sorts of prizes. That's how he came to this country – to enter a tango contest. He won First Place, decided to stay, and wants to become a citizen."

"Good for him." Hallie's brain was racing. "Was Fernando still in the gang? Was Rhoda's timing wrong? Could Carlie be the person he killed? If he'd trained to become a pharmacist, wouldn't he know about poisons?

Checking her watch, Hallie asked to use the bathroom. Once inside, she slipped on her gloves, and quietly lifted a squashed Band-Aid box and a used-up Grecian Formula tube from the waste basket. She dropped them into a plastic bag in her purse, then flushed, and washed her hands.

"You were most kind to see me," she said, moments later, as her host walked her to the door.

"Let's hope I helped a teeny bit. You can certainly cross Fernando off your list of suspects."

Hallie smiled and stepped into the elevator. "Thanks Rhoda. I'll remember that."

## — Chapter 85 —

LATER that afternoon, Hallie kept her word and called TB to report her visit to Rhoda. As she relayed their conversation (except for the part about Fernando killing someone), she realized that Rhoda hadn't helped her lover's case at all. Intentionally or otherwise, she had almost confirmed him as a suspect. Was she planning to break off the relationship?

Grateful for Hallie's call, TB shared the news that Dr.

Toy's staff had located the mysterious hammer, and despite his skepticism, sent it to the lab for tests.

The detective was surprisingly supportive when Hallie asked if she could bring him Rhoda's waste basket treasures so they could extract Fernando's DNA and fingerprints.

"But hold onto them for now," he said. "I'll let you know if we need them."

In the meantime, TB reported, Herb Gaines was turning nasty, and threatening a lawsuit. TB had talked to Nate Garchik. Since they had narrowed their suspects down to Jeff, Fernando, and Herb Gaines, and felt they were closing in on the truth, they agreed to pay Gaines' living expenses – temporarily – in return for holding off the suit.

— Chapter 86 —

TWO DAYS LATER, on a Wednesday in late July, Sam Butler returned from New York with the happy news that his daughter's wedding went well, that he was deeply in love, and that Margot had agreed to move in with him. Hallie was thrilled.

Her afternoon mail brought an announcement of Polly Jane Hodges' marriage and a note with the couple's new address. They had moved to San Jose, and would love to see their friends once they got settled.

The next night, Margot had a rehearsal, Cas was still traveling, and Sam invited Hallie to dinner to "catch up" on the investigation.

"You look fantastic!" were her first words when they

met in a booth at Osteria, a neighborhood restaurant. "Love agrees with you."

"So does losing ten pounds," he said, laughing. "Margot's a health nut, as you know. I haven't had any red meat for weeks. Tonight I'm going to cheat."

"I'll never tell. By the way, did you know Tobias sold the dance school?"

"Good for him. I wasn't planning to go back. Margot says she just wants me to get smoochy when we dance. She doesn't care what my feet do."

The waiter took their orders and brought wine. After clinking glasses, Hallie recounted all that had happened in his absence, including her visit with Rhoda.

"You didn't tell TB that Fernando had killed someone?" he asked. "Why not?"

"It's hearsay, Sam. Maybe Fernando was bragging, maybe Rhoda got it wrong, who knows? I'm afraid that if TB heard that statement, he might feel he had to investigate. Fernando could lose his job, probably his citizenship, and it'd be a big mess, all because he told his lover something in confidence."

"You're right." He nodded. "What about that necklace? Do you really care what a psychic said?"

"Goodness, you scientists are as cynical as journalists. Even Cas thinks Zlotta is pretty observant. All she said was that the beads seemed familiar. Since we don't have any other clues, why not take a closer look?"

"What kind of beads were they?"

"Hard red shells with a black dot – they looked like ladybugs. Fernando said he'd bought them in South America

– Suriname, I think. He called them 'rosary beads' but the necklace wasn't a rosary."

"Have you checked online?"

"No – frankly, I didn't think of it."

At that point, the waiter set down two plates of steaming spaghetti. Hallie grinned. "Meat sauce doesn't count as meat, Sam. Enjoy your food, then you can tell me all about – oops, excuse me!"

The voice on her cell belonged to Cas, saying he was surprising her and coming home a day early. She was delighted, stayed to hear Sam's tale of love, then gave him a hug and drove to the airport.

## — Chapter 87 —

ONCE SAFELY HOME, Cas, still on Eastern time, set down his briefcase, laptop and bag, and began to shed his clothes. Hallie hurried down the hall to her computer, determined to try to identify the "damn beads."

After a half hour of frustration, she put her computer to sleep just as Cas came in to say goodnight.

"What's wrong?" he asked, seeing her face.

"I've tried everything," she groaned. "I Googled 'rosary beads' and got, well, rosary beads. They don't look anything like Rhoda's. I tried 'beads – Suriname' and 'necklace beads' and 'exotic necklace beads' and everything else I could think of. Nothing. Guess I'm just exhausted."

"Me, too." He smiled and kissed her forehead. "Let me sit there a minute?"

"Be my guest."

He slid into her chair. "What else should I know about the beads?"

"They look sort of like ladybugs. But 'ladybug beads' brought up a lot of glass ladybug beads."

"Are they red? Anything distinctive about them?"

"Red – with a black spot at the bottom."

"Okay, hold on." Clicking on Google, he typed in "red beads with black spots" and hit Enter.

Hallie yawned. "We should both go to bed, darling."

"Patience, my sweet." Up popped a list of possible leads. Cas scrolled down the screen and stopped cold at a title: "*Hundreds of 'deadly' seed bracelets recalled.*"

He clicked on it, and read aloud from a newswire: "*Native jewelry recalled after Grace's Gift Shop in Peru reveals it contains highly toxic seeds.*"

The picture showed a bracelet made of scarlet beads with black dots.

"Oh, my God!" Hallie gasped, staring over his shoulder. "Those look exactly like her necklace!"

Cas read on: "*This decorative bead, made from the jequirity bean often known as 'rosary pea,' is the lethal seed of the plant Abrus Precatorius. It contains abrin, a controlled substance under the U.S. Terrorism Act. Abrin can kill if just 3 micrograms are inhaled or swallowed, 75 times less than a fatal dose of ricin, to which it's related.*"

"Scary stuff," Cas mumbled to his stunned wife.

He continued: "*A woody vine native to Suriname, Abrus Precatorius is also known throughout the tropics for its remarkable medicinal qualities. Fortunately, the shells of the seeds, extremely poisonous if opened, are difficult to shatter.*"

Hallie gulped, "The hammer!"

"*Symptoms of poisoning may take several days to appear. They include acute gastroenteritis, nausea, vomiting, diarrhea, and eventual fatal kidney failure.*"

"Those were Carlie's symptoms – exactly!"

"*People who purchased any form of jewelry made from these beads are asked to bag the piece in plastic, seal it securely, wash your hands with strong soap and disinfectant, and don't touch any part of your body. Bring the bag back to the store where you bought it for a full refund.*"

Cas exhaled loudly. "Looks like you may have struck gold – thanks to your psychic noticing the necklace. I'll never knock psychics again."

He saved the article and shut down the computer. "Let's pack it in for now, honey. If you Google 'abrin' in the morning, I think you'll find all the info you need."

## — Chapter 88 —

SHORTLY AFTER NINE the next day, Hallie called Dr. Toy. Told that the medical examiner was busy, she insisted that the matter was urgent.

After a long wait, he came on the line. "What's so important, Hallie?" His tone was slightly resentful.

"Sorry, Dr. Toy. But I think I know what killed Carlie Gaines and Mario Ingoli. Have you heard of a poison called abrin?"

"Certainly! It's one of the deadliest toxins known. It's in the ricin family. Our test was negative."

"You tested for ricin. What about abrin?"

"We assumed the test included –" He stopped him-self. "What makes you think it was abrin?"

"I'm hoping there's evidence on that hammer you got from Mr. Ingoli's workshop."

"Hammer? Oh, yes, I'm awaiting results – although TB said the possibility of finding poison on it was negligible. He was just humoring you."

She frowned. "Well, please humor me some more. I think you may find traces of abrin on that hammer along with fingerprints, perhaps those of a dance instructor."

"Oh?" His tone was softening. "What you're suggest-ing is quite possible. Considering the symptoms, the delayed onset, the bodies turning blue. Abrin could very well have caused those two deaths. Do you realize how lethal that toxin is?"

"Yes, I've read up on it."

"The amount on the tip of a pin could kill you – by inhalation or ingestion. You don't fool around with it. Do you have any idea of the source?"

"It might be…a woman's necklace made of rosary pea beads."

"Here in San Francisco?"

"Yes, she and her boyfriend – he's a suspect in Carlie's murder – have an apartment in Pacific Heights."

"Email me his name and address right away and tell TB what's happening. If you're correct, there could still be some abrin there. We can't take chances. I'm sending the hazmat team and notifying emergency services. Promise me you won't go anywhere near that building?"

"I've absolutely no intention of going there," she said,

startled by his strong reaction.

"Send me that address!"

He slammed down the phone.

— Chapter 89 —

"WHY ARE YOU WASTING the coroner's time?" demanded an irate TB, moments later.

"I'm not," Hallie retorted. "Dr. Toy sounds really scared. Will you listen for a minute?"

"Yeah. Talk."

"Okay. I first noticed Rhoda's necklace in the dance class picture." (TB would discount everything if he knew a psychic was involved.)

"The beads were distinctive. I was stumped at first. Fernando called them 'rosary beads,' but I was finally able to identify them as rosary *pea* seeds. They contain a deadly toxin called abrin. It takes a strong blow to crack open the seed to get to the abrin, but it would take less than a pinhead of the poison to kill a person. And the symptoms of abrin poisoning match both Carlie's and Ingoli's bodies."

"Dr. Toy said that?"

"Yes. So if the coroner confirms that they died from abrin, and finds abrin and Fernando's prints on the hammer, that's pretty conclusive, isn't it?"

"Circumstantial at best." But the detective was concerned. "Toy has to let us know ASAP if there's poison on the hammer, and whose prints – if any – he finds there. You say Rhoda and Fernando are living together? Maybe Fernando did kill Carlie. Maybe Rhoda helped him do it.

Maybe Fernando meant to kill Rhoda. Who knows? Maybe Toy won't find anything on the hammer. *Nothing's* conclusive at this point."

"Dr. Toy says the poison's so dangerous, he's sending a hazmat team to get the necklace and check the apartment for traces of abrin."

"What? Why didn't you tell me? That's a local emergency! We may have to empty the building. I'll get right on it. And Hallie, don't even *think* of going there!" Click.

## — Chapter 90 —

IGNORING ALL WARNINGS, Hallie tried to drive by the apartment on the way to her downtown office; fire trucks, police cars and other emergency vehicles, however, had blocked the street.

Once back in her office, she immersed herself in work, trying to engage her mind as well as catch up on her neglected correspondence. Lately, she'd been pondering the changes in her industry.

Like so many revered institutions, the Public Relations world not only had to keep up with the social media, but also, with the constant influx of new technologies and software. Her clients expected it, and as she told Cas when he asked why she worked so hard, "If I don't stay current, my competitors will grind me into meatballs."

Not too surprisingly, Cas had begun encouraging her to sell her "bleeping business" so they could have more time together. Her late father's trust fund covered her needs and more; sleuthing was taking much of her time, her PR clients were dwindling, and her pro bono work was almost useless, since most nonprofits would rather have a check.

Cas's gentle nudging didn't upset her. She knew it came from love, concern for her health, and his desire to start a family. He reminded her, too, that she no longer needed to prove herself; she was so much more than a "rich socialite."

Slowly, in fact, the idea of changing her life was sounding more and more appealing.

— Chapter 91 —

That afternoon, TB phoned his anxious helper. His tone was warmer. "Good news, Hallie. The coroner's team found the necklace in the apartment and you were right – those beads *are* seeds – 'rosary pea' seeds – and they're as deadly as you can get. They scare the hell out of everyone."

"Including me."

"Microscopic examination of the necklace showed that someone removed a single bead, but there was no sign of it – or the poison – in any of the rooms."

"Were Rhoda and Fernando home?"

"No, the building manager let the hazmat team in. The necklace was in a drawer with lots of junk jewelry – no pearls or diamonds or anything that looked real."

"Dr. Toy told you that?"

"Yup. Said he was revising the death certificates. His toxicology expert tested the victims' blood and tissues, and concluded that both parties died of systemic poisoning caused by ingestion or inhalation of abrin."

"How awful! Had they known what it was, maybe they could have been saved."

"No, there's no antidote for abrin. Toy said the untouched seeds could pass through the GI tract without harm, but not the ones with necklace holes. Yet how would you get someone to swallow one of those hard-shelled beads?"

"You wouldn't."

"Precisely. In order to extract even the minute amount needed, the killer would've had to break it open."

"With a hammer."

"You're way ahead of me. Hallie. Toy *did* find a tiny trace of abrin on the tool – and two sets of prints. He sent them over. One is Mario Ingoli's – they match the victim's fingers. The other isn't in the system. Whoever used the hammer apparently soaked it in bleach, but missed an infinitesimal bit between the prongs. Then he carefully wrapped the hammer in plastic and threw it in the garbage, where Ingoli had the misfortune to discover and retrieve it."

"And that second set of prints could be Fernando's."

"Or anyone's. But as I said, they're not in our data base. How long would it take you to bring me the treasures you pulled out of Fernando's waste basket? I'll send them to the lab with a 'rush', and hopefully, they'll get the prints back to us before they close for the weekend."

"Give me fifteen minutes," she said.

## — Chapter 92 —

TWENTY MINUTES LATER, Hallie sat in TB's office. He had just sent the crushed Band-Aid box and Grecian Formula tube to the lab with a "RUSH!" stamp.

"Do you mind if I sit here and wait for the results?" she asked. "I brought a book to read."

"Not at all." He sank into a chair behind his desk. "Don't quote me, I don't want you stealing my job. But you've been surprisingly helpful on this homicide."

"You *do* have a sense of humor," she teased. "Your job's pretty safe. I don't know why I felt so strongly about this case. Guess I sort of identified with Carlie."

"Understandably. Let's talk a minute. What do we have so far?"

"Well, if Fernando's prints match those on the hammer, that would tell us that he was rejected by Carlie, desperate to buy the dance school, and knew that the beads he gave Rhoda were poisonous. He took a hammer, split one open, and very carefully removed it from the necklace. But how did he get the poison to Carlie?"

"Good question."

"When will we hear from your lab?"

"Soon, I hope. But we mustn't go with the obvious. We still have Jeff Donegan, rejected by Carlie, and bidding against her to buy the school. Did you know he served a year in prison for larceny?"

"No," said Hallie. "But he lies and makes a sport of seducing married women. He has no morals. I'm not surprised."

180

"Then we have Carlie's not-so-dear daddy, Herb Gaines. She paid him to stay out of her life. As long as she was alive, he had no claim on her money and no source of income. Now he claims he's her rightful heir."

"Fernando was also rejected by Carlie," Hallie added, "and may have killed her because she was his biggest competitor for the school." After a short pause, she continued, "I didn't mention this, but Fernando told his girlfriend Rhoda that he killed someone in Peru. Or so she says."

TB shrugged. "Hearsay. What about Tobias?"

"Tobias had no motive. He wasn't rejected by Carlie and he was about to get big bucks from her for the school."

"The lawyer?"

"Nate Garchik loved and planned to marry Carlie. He had his jeweler make special wedding rings. He showed them to me. He couldn't have faked the grief I saw."

"But isn't he in charge of distributing her assets? Doesn't he get a percentage of her estate?"

"Yes, TB, but he was already a wealthy man. He doesn't need her money."

At that moment, the detective's partner appeared. "The lab thought you might want this."

"Well done, Lenny." TB tore open the envelope and read its contents. "Hallie," he said, breaking into a grin, "We have a match."

She glanced at the paper and smiled back. "Just as I thought."

## — Chapter 93 —

THE FRIDAY EVENING tango class was in full session when Hallie, TB, and Lenny quietly entered the ballroom.

Twenty women and four men stood watching Fernando and a comely blonde demonstrate steps.

"He's a joy to watch," whispered Hallie. "He makes it look so easy."

Fernando was shouting over the music. "You see how she lean back? The man always keep knees bent. Now, everyone take partner."

As soon as the piece ended, TB pulled the cord on the disc player. Surprise silenced the crowd. The officer flashed his badge and raised his hands for attention.

"Class is over," he announced firmly. "You're all free to leave. I'm sure the school will give you credit for this lesson."

"What ees?" A furious Fernando came storming up to the intruders. "What you do here? What you tell my class?"

"This is a homicide investigation, Mr. Ruiz. We need to talk to you."

"Why me?"

"Because we think you might have some information about Carlie Gaines' murder."

"Carlie?" He seemed shocked.

TB reached into his back pocket. "Read him his rights, Lenny. I've got the cuffs."

"You have the right to remain silent –"

"No!" Fernando screamed, just as Rhoda bustled up.

"Why are you arresting this man?" she demanded.

"Hold on," said Hallie glancing around the room. The students were all staring, fascinated. "TB?"

He followed her eyes and caught her meaning. "You're all ordered to leave," he told the crowd. "Now!"

Lenny helped usher out the students, then closed the door behind them.

Rhoda's finger to her lips signaled Fernando not to talk. "What is all this nonsense?" she asked TB. "You have no right to interrupt this class. Fernando could sue you."

"Glad to meet you, too, Mrs. Starr-Stevens. I'm detective –"

"Ees okay, sweetheart," interrupted Fernando, trying to be calm. "I tell them I know nothing, they let me go."

"Don't tell them anything! I'm getting you a lawyer."

"I don't need lawyer! I tell truth. They let me go."

"Do we have to arrest you, too?" Lenny reached into his pocket.

"No cuffs, Lenny," said TB. "Perhaps Mrs. Starr-Stevens will be good enough to accompany us to the station while we question Mr. Ruiz."

— Chapter 94 —

HALLIE took her now-familiar place outside the Interrogation Room, peering through the one-way glass. Police Lieutenant Helen Kaiser, TB's Supervisor, stood beside her and turned up the sound.

Inside, Lenny positioned himself by the door. Fernando sat in the suspect's seat, with Rhoda next to him, where lawyers usually sit. She reached for his hand and held it.

"Let's all be calm," TB said, as he took a chair opposite the pair. "We're hoping you can give us some answers."

"What you want to know?" asked Fernando, still hostile.

"Patience, please. Let me tell you briefly what we do know. Carlie Gaines died from ingestion of a deadly poison called abrin. Have you heard of it?"

Both shook their heads.

"Let me refresh your memory. On your South American cruise, you stopped in a city called Suriname. You bought some native jewelry. Do you recall that?"

Fernando shook his head. "I no remember."

"Of course you do," said Rhoda. "That's where you bought me the lovely necklace."

"Oh, *si, si* – the rosary beads."

"Rosary *pea* beads," corrected TB. "Did you know the beads contain that poison I mentioned?"

"Oh, yes, the man tell us beads have poison."

"But he said they're perfectly safe as long as I don't swallow them," Rhoda volunteered. "I told him I didn't usually swallow my jewelry. He also said they have healing properties."

"Mr. Ruiz," said Lenny, moving in closer. "Did you know that a hazardous materials team searched your apartment this morning?"

Rhoda bristled. "Of course we knew! They searched the whole building and tracked dirt on my new carpet. The building manager didn't know what they were looking for

184

and said that whatever it was they didn't find it."

"Oh, but they did, Mrs. Starr-Stevens. They found your necklace with the poisonous beads."

"They took my necklace?"

"Yes, with one bead missing – and some bleach stains on the string."

"I have no idea what you're talking about. That's the way we bought it."

"No, *cara*," said Fernando. "The necklace perfect when we buy, remember? We look very close."

Rhoda pulled away her hand. "Don't listen to him. He's having memory problems. What's this all about, detective?"

"Those beads contain a lethal poison…the kind that killed Carlie Gaines."

"Surely you can't think I had anything to do with it." Her anger was growing. "I hate to say this, but Fernando's the one who wanted her dead. He was sure she was the reason he couldn't buy the school. Ask him about the beads."

"*Cara*, what you say? I know nothing about beads! I love Carlie! She was wonderful woman with beautiful soul. I never hurt her. I love her." Tears streamed down his face.

All eyes turned to Rhoda.

"Don't look at me," she snapped. "What motive could I possibly have? You think I could be jealous of a stupid tango dancer? He's my gigolo. He takes me places I couldn't go to alone. Besides, I had nothing against Carlie. Why would I kill her?"

"Fingerprints don't lie," said TB.

'Fingerprints? On my own beads?"

"No." TB reached into his briefcase and drew out a plastic wrapped hammer. "On this – you might call it the murder weapon."

Rhoda stared, pale as a sheet. "Th – that's not mine," she stammered. "My hammer went into the garbage. I saw the truck go off with it!" Her hand clapped her mouth as she realized what she'd said. "What I mean is –"

"A garbage collector died because of that hammer," TB said quietly. "It had traces of abrin on it."

"Fernando gave me that hammer! He said to get rid of it!"

"I don't think so, ma'am. There were only two sets of prints on the hammer. One was the garbage collector's. The other was yours."

## — Chapter 95 —

IT WAS AFTER MIDNIGHT when Hallie finally came home, exhausted, and crawled into bed, hoping not to wake her husband.

"You're back." Cas groaned, and opened a sleepy eye to check the wall clock. "What took you so long?"

"I'm sorry," she said, kissing his cheek. "TB had me write out everything I could remember, then feed it into the computer, then go over it twice, then call Nate Garchik, Carlie's lawyer, and wrap it all up."

"What did Garchik have to say?"

"He was just glad it was over and he could settle with Herb Gaines. He's going to pay him a monthly allowance rather than a lump sum the guy could lose in a poker game.

Meantime, TB let Fernando go. The poor guy was scratching his head and trying to figure out what hit him. Meantime, Rhoda's being charged with two murders: first degree in Carlie's case, and involuntary manslaughter in the death of the poor garbage collector."

Cas reached under the covers and pulled his wife towards him. "Thanks for calling to let me know you'd be late. I was beginning to worry."

"You were not, you were snoring away."

"That was the dog."

"We don't have a dog."

"Picky, picky. Tell me – when did you first suspect Rhoda?"

She moved slightly back to look at him. "Remember I told you I had tea – well, actually hot water – with Fernando? Then he walked me to my car, blew me a kiss and drifted off. I was just starting the motor when I saw Rhoda sitting in the passenger's seat of a car – she must've had a driver – watching us. I suddenly realized how insanely jealous she was."

"Go on."

"Jeff told me that Carlie couldn't stand Fernando – said he always smelled sweaty. But Carlie flirted with Fernando because she hoped to buy the school and wanted to keep him as an instructor. Even Jeff, who hates Fernando's guts, admits he's a fabulous dancer."

"Is he?"

"If I say yes, will you be insanely jealous?"

"That's twice you've used that phrase. I could never be a cliché. Your feet are cold."

"I know. Anyway, I was confused when I went to see Rhoda. I still thought the killer might be Fernando. I took the old tube of hair stuff because I knew it would have his prints, then I decided to take the Band-Aid box, too. It had a lipstick smudge so I was pretty sure it would have Rhoda's prints."

"And it did."

"Yes. When TB confronted Rhoda with the evidence, she tried to blame Fernando. TB told her some lie about finding bleach on the strand, and she finally confessed, insisting that she never wanted to kill Carlie. She thought the abrin would just get her a little sick so she'd stop flirting with Fernando. Also, it would give him time to buy the school – with Rhoda's money, of course. The school would be in her name, so her 'gigolo' would be forever beholden to her."

"We poor males are no match for a clever female. How'd she get Carlie to take the poison?"

"Simple. Apparently it's tasteless. She put a teeny bit on a Hershey's chocolate kiss, rewrapped it in its foil, and passed a dish of kisses around to the Zumba class, making sure Carlie got the bad one."

"One should never accept kisses from strange women."

"I'll remember that." Hallie cuddled up to him. "Let's go to sleep."

"You haven't finished. Was TB grateful to you?"

"In a way. But he made me promise to take care of you and not bug him anymore this year. So I promised I'd spend more time with you. I may even sell my business."

"What great news!"

"I have another surprise for you, too."

"Uh-oh. Dare I ask?"

"Sure."

"Is it bigger than a bread box?"

"It will be some day. It starts out small."

"It?"

"Well, it may be a he, and it may be a she."

Cas's eyes widened. "Are you telling me –"

"Yes, sweetheart. I was going to save it for tomorrow, but it just popped out, so to speak. You're the first to know. Well, second, actually. Well, third, if you must know. Zlotta told me months ago that I'd be a mommy next year."

"Honestly? Congratulations, my beautiful mommy!" He hugged her tightly. "I'm ecstatic – I can't believe it. Are you okay? Does the doctor know? Do we have to name her Zlotta Casserly?"

"Only if she's a girl."

"That's a relief. Shall we break out the champagne?"

"Sorry, I can't have booze."

"Thank goodness. I'm thrilled beyond words, but we put the magazine to bed this evening and I'm totally wiped out. You're not going to have any of those funny whims, like wanting a sausage pizza at three in the morning, are you?"

"Why, yes, thank you. It's not even one, and I'd kill for a chocolate macaroon."

"You serious?"

"Completely. But let's go to sleep, anyway, darling. I need you to warm my toes."

CPSIA information can be obtained at www.ICGtesting.com
Printed in the USA
LVOW081548060513

332504LV00002B/73/P